NEW SURGEON
AT ASHVALE A&E

BY
JOANNA NEIL

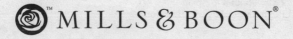

MILLS & BOON®

All the characters in this book have no existence outside the imagination of the author, and have no relation whatsoever to anyone bearing the same name or names. They are not even distantly inspired by any individual known or unknown to the author, and all the incidents are pure invention.

All Rights Reserved including the right of reproduction in whole or in part in any form. This edition is published by arrangement with Harlequin Enterprises II BV/S.à.r.l. The text of this publication or any part thereof may not be reproduced or transmitted in any form or by any means, electronic or mechanical, including photocopying, recording, storage in an information retrieval system, or otherwise, without the written permission of the publisher.

This book is sold subject to the condition that it shall not, by way of trade or otherwise, be lent, resold, hired out or otherwise circulated without the prior consent of the publisher in any form of binding or cover other than that in which it is published and without a similar condition including this condition being imposed on the subsequent purchaser.

® and TM are trademarks owned and used by the trademark owner and/or its licensee. Trademarks marked with ® are registered with the United Kingdom Patent Office and/or the Office for Harmonisation in the Internal Market and in other countries.

First published in Great Britain 2010
Harlequin Mills & Boon Limited,
Eton House, 18-24 Paradise Road, Richmond, Surrey TW9 1SR

© Joanna Neil 2010

ISBN: 978 0 263 87688 8

Harlequin Mills & Boon policy is to use papers that are natural, renewable and recyclable products and made from wood grown in sustainable forests. The logging and manufacturing process conform to the legal environmental regulations of the country of origin.

Printed and bound in Spain
by Litografia Rosés, S.A., Barcelona

NEW SURGEON
AT ASHVALE A&E

CHAPTER ONE

'WELL, poppet, here we are at last. A little later than I'd planned, but at least we've arrived.' Ruby made a neat turn into the parking slot in the hospital grounds and turned off the ignition. From the rear of the car, a response came in the form of a soft gurgle, and she swivelled around to gaze for a moment at the baby. Becky was lying contentedly in her car seat, blowing bubbles while doing her best to grasp her toes with her fingers.

Smiling, Ruby slid out of the driver's seat and went around to the rear of the vehicle to retrieve the infant.

'It's a good thing you're such a happy soul,' she murmured. 'It makes life so much easier. After all, much as I love you, I hadn't planned on bringing you with me today.'

Becky wriggled, her arms, legs and whole body moving in excited anticipation, a beaming smile lighting her chubby face at the prospect of her aunt coming close.

Ruby began to unclip the seat restraint. 'I've no idea where your mother could have disappeared to,' she said softly, 'and yet she promised me faithfully that she would come and fetch you so that I could go along to my meeting.' She lifted her palms in a questioning gesture. 'But where is she? I haven't a clue. Your guess is as good as mine.'

Becky chuckled, her blue eyes bright, as Ruby lifted the

child seat out of the car. 'As for you, you don't have a care in the world, do you, little one?' Ruby smiled indulgently. 'What does it matter to you that I have to go and listen to my new boss challenge us to cut costs to the bone and find all sorts of impossible ways of doing it? And what's he doing there anyway taking my place? I had my name pinned on that job, and I'm pretty sure I would have made things work for us without any of this argy-bargy and bad feeling.'

Becky studied her, a small frown appearing on the soft skin of her brow, as though she was trying very hard to make sense of the flow of words. Ruby laughed softly. 'Yes, I know. Your auntie's as mad as a hatter. Why else would she be going to a conference with a baby in tow?' She leaned over and tickled the child, her chestnut-coloured hair falling in a silky swathe about her shoulders. Becky giggled and grasped a handful of hair.

'Ow…ow…ow,' Ruby exclaimed, pretending to be caught.

'Mum…mm…mum.' Six-month-old Becky blew raspberries from her pink lips and cooed, finally letting go of Ruby's hair and beginning to suck on a small fist.

'Yes, you're absolutely right,' Ruby murmured, straightening up. 'Your mum's not herself these days, and we just have to try to make the best of things, don't we? When all's said and done, we can probably slip in quietly somewhere near the back of the room. With any luck, no one will even notice that I've brought an uninvited guest along with me.'

By now she was approaching the main entrance of the hospital. People were coming and going, hurrying through the doors that continually swished open and closed. Some were dressed casually, visiting their relatives who were unfortunate enough to be hospitalised, perhaps, while one or two were more formally attired—doctors, maybe, or people who had appointments with consultants within the hospital.

Others, presumably taking a break in the warm afternoon

sunshine, were sitting or standing to one side by a well tended shrub garden, breathing in the fresh air.

Suddenly, the doors opened up once more, and a man lumbered towards her, head down, a disgruntled expression on his face. Perhaps the collision that followed was inevitable. Either way, he slammed into Ruby with some force, so that she swung to one side and momentarily lost her balance. She kept a firm grip on the baby chair as it carved a wild arc through the air, and all the while her one thought was to protect the infant. Becky began to cry, frightened by the sudden jolt, and for a second or two, Ruby was afraid that she might have been hurt.

At the same time she was aware of pain slicing through her wrist, and as she fought to regain her balance, she realised that the man had rushed away, leaving her only with the impression of a scowling, grim countenance.

'Are you all right?' A man's voice cut into her thoughts, the deep, warm tones edged with a drizzle of honey that smoothed over her shattered nerves. 'Is the baby okay?' He reached out and lightly grasped her arm, steadying her, at the same time laying a hand on the baby seat to ensure that it was safe.

'I think so.' Disorientated, she set the carrier down on the ground, checking swiftly that all was well with Becky. 'Everything's fine, baby,' she murmured, reassuring the infant and distracting her with a brightly coloured teething ring that jangled and provided endless possibilities for exploration. 'She seems to be none the worse for it.' Then, once she was satisfied that the baby was safe, she looked up into the eyes of the man who had come to her aid.

They were beautiful eyes, a curious mixture of blue and grey, reminding her strangely of sea mist and sun-dappled water, and at the same time invoking a disturbing reaction within her, a strange restlessness that she hadn't encountered in a long, long time.

She pulled herself together and straightened up, leaving the carrier where it was for the time being so that Becky would have an opportunity to examine her new toy and forget all about the incident. That left her free to rub gently at her wrist where it had been wrenched.

'I have a feeling I might have seen that man somewhere before,' she told him, frowning a little. 'I can't quite place him, and I only caught a glimpse, but there was something about him that was familiar.'

'Really? He didn't look too happy, did he? Maybe things hadn't gone quite the way he expected in there.' He looked towards the building, then glanced back at her, noting the way she was surreptitiously soothing her jarred wrist. 'Do you think someone should take a look at that?'

'No, it'll be fine, thanks.' She gave a short laugh. 'Anyway, I'm in the right place if I change my mind, aren't I? A&E is just around the corner.'

'That's true.' A serious expression settled on his face as he appeared to ponder the wisdom of leaving things be, and she took a moment or two to study him more thoroughly.

He was way too smartly dressed to be a casual visitor to the hospital, or even a patient, she guessed. He wasn't wearing a doctor's name badge, so it was possible he was someone from a pharmaceutical company here to meet up with their chief pharmacist and his team. Ruby knew the hospital chiefs were worried about the drugs bill, and meetings were planned to discuss the issue.

He was wearing a suit, the immaculate, dark grey jacket sitting easily on broad shoulders, while the trousers fitted him to perfection, outlining a washboard-flat stomach and long, strong legs. Altogether, he made an immediate, disturbing impact on her.

'Do you need any help to get to where you need to be? Perhaps I could carry the child for you?' He was watching her closely, his gaze skimming over her, taking in her casual summer clothes, a button-through cotton top and gently flowing skirt, before coming to rest once more on her face.

She blinked, trying to pull her thoughts back on track. She shook her head. 'No, thanks all the same. I'll manage.' She smiled. 'Besides, I expect you have places you need to be...unless you'd finished your business here?' Why else would he have been standing outside the hospital? He looked like a man who would be continually on the move, energetic, a force to be reckoned with. Perhaps it was the suit that gave her that impression. It somehow denoted a businesslike demeanour, a man at the height of his profession.

'You're right. I was just taking a break for a while, enjoying the sunshine and the cooling breeze. Hospitals can seem like soulless places at times, can't they, even here in beautiful Buckinghamshire?'

'That's true.' She nodded. 'I wasn't much looking forward to coming here today, but unfortunately I have a meeting to go to.'

He frowned. 'Is that so? Nothing badly wrong, I hope—with you or the baby?'

She made a wry face. 'Nothing at all. I'm fighting fit, and so is Becky, which is just as well, since I have to go and do battle, so to speak. It won't do to let the chiefs have everything their own way.'

A puzzled look crossed his features, and it seemed as though he expected her to say more, but she didn't try to explain any further. 'I must go,' she said. 'I'm late already. Thanks very much for coming to help me. I do appreciate it.'

She had delayed long enough, and the meeting must be well under way by now. If she hurried, there was still time to make her presence felt. She picked up the baby carrier and, with a nod in his direction, she walked swiftly into the building.

James and Olivia, two senior house officers from her

team, met her at the door to the room where the meeting was taking place.

'Thank heaven you made it at last,' Olivia said. 'We were beginning to think you would never get here.' She turned to greet Becky with a smile, picking up the baby's rattle and gently waving it in front of the child, so that the infant tried to grab it and pull it to her mouth. Olivia laughed softly. 'Okay, okay, you can have it. I was just teasing.' She turned back to Ruby. 'Everyone's taking a break for coffee just now. We had to stop for a while…emotions were threatening to boil over.'

'So I gathered.' Ruby's expression was sombre. 'Is the new man making his presence felt?'

'Oh, yes.' James nodded. Lean and fit-looking, with dark brown hair that was cut in a short, neat style, he was an energetic, efficient colleague. 'He's definitely on the side of the board. Cuts, cuts and more cuts. That seems to be his mantra. That's why I called you. I couldn't believe you weren't going to be here to argue our corner.' He led the way towards the back of the room. 'Some of the senior managers look as though they've been up half the night working out what they can chop next. The trust is in so much debt that they say drastic measures are called for.'

'I wanted to be here right from the beginning,' Ruby said. 'You know I did…only I agreed to look after Becky while my sister went to see the doctor at the local surgery. There would have been plenty of time for me to come to the meeting afterwards, except that Sophie didn't come home to take over from me. I waited and waited, and then I got to wondering whether there was any point in my coming along and saying anything at all at the meeting. After all, the new man is the one who'll be making all the decisions from now on.'

'And that was where the management made their big mistake.' Olivia frowned. 'You should have been the one to take charge, we all know that. You've been the mainstay of the A&E department for years, keeping things running smoothly while the boss readied himself for retirement. This job should have been the reward for all your hard work.'

Ruby made a wry smile. 'Well, in the end it hasn't happened, and there's no use crying over spilt milk. Management have chosen the man they feel best to put all their changes into place.' She gave a soft chuckle. 'Perhaps they thought things would become a bit too contentious if they put me in charge. I wouldn't have accepted that their way was the only way.'

'More than likely. So what happened with Sophie?' Olivia asked. 'She must have known this was important to you.'

Ruby frowned. 'I'm not sure. I was looking forward to hearing how things had gone at the surgery, but when she didn't come back, I started to worry. Something must have gone wrong…but maybe I should have expected that. She's definitely not herself these days. She's not been well for quite some time, and I've been trying to persuade her for ages to go for some tests so that we can find out exactly what's wrong. I suspect it's a hormonal problem, with her body chemistry being out of synch ever since Becky was born, but she wouldn't let me do anything to help. I was so pleased when I finally managed to get her to agree to go and talk to our GP.'

The SHOs nodded. 'But something obviously didn't go to plan?' Olivia pointed out some available seats and they went to take their places.

Ruby shook her head. 'I rang the surgery to see if she'd turned up there, and apparently she did, but then she didn't wait for her appointment. I've absolutely no idea where she might be. I've tried ringing her, but she's not answering her phone. Anything could have happened. She's just not thinking clearly these days. I dare say I'll find out later what went wrong.'

'I'm glad you made it in the end, anyway,' James murmured. 'You of all people should be able to make the bosses see sense here. The way things are going, they'll walk rough-shod over all of us. How on earth do they expect us to give a viable service to the local area if they plan to get rid of staff and close units?'

'I think that's the least of their worries.' Ruby set the baby down on the floor and glanced around as people began to troop back into the room. 'What about the new boss, anyway? What's he like? Has he not managed to come up with any reasonable suggestions?'

'You have to be kidding.' Olivia gave a short, humourless laugh. 'He may well be an A&E doctor, but he's management through and through, and *reasonable* isn't in their vocabulary. No one seems to be paying any attention to what the people at the sharp end, those who actually have to do all the work, have to say.'

'We'll just have to do what we can to make them see sense.' Ruby moved restlessly in her seat, then ran a hand through the length of her burnished hair, lifting it away from her nape to let a cool waft of air fan her heated skin. 'It's so warm in here,' she commented, 'with all that sunshine pouring in through the windows.'

She reached into the large linen bag she had brought with her and fished out the printed programme for the meeting. 'Maybe this will do the trick.' She leaned back in her seat and began to fan herself lightly with the paper.

'Oh, that's so much better.' She murmured her apprecia-tion of the cool drift of air just as she became aware of a still-ness settling in the room. Glancing around, she saw that most of the board members had taken their places on the dais, while one seat remained empty.

A man came through a side door just then and strode pur-posefully across the back of the room. He turned into the corridor between the mass of seats, passing her just at the moment when she tilted her head back and lightly blew the tendrils of hair away from her brow. Becky gurgled content-edly, and he glanced briefly in their direction.

Ruby's eyes widened, her senses responding to his presence with a faint frisson of dismay. His tall, lean figure was instantly familiar to her. He had that coolly confident air of a man who was in command of all he surveyed, the measured look of a man who was in control at all times. It was that suit that said it all, along with his authoritative demeanour, the assured way that he moved without faltering towards his goal.

His dark brows made an infinitesimal upward lift as he looked her over, and his expression showed…what was it…? Disbelief…recognition…along with a soupcon of amuse-ment. There was definitely an element of wry humour in that glance, cleverly disguised so as not to be obvious, but it was there, all the same, in the faint twist at the corner of his mouth and in the dancing gleam in his blue-grey eyes.

Ruby stared at him, following his progress as he walked along the aisle and sprang up the steps to the dais with lithe ease. He took his seat at the table alongside the board members.

She frowned, dark brows meeting in her normally unfur-rowed brow. Surely he wasn't her new boss? A sinking feeling in the pit of her stomach told her that he most likely was.

She pushed the programme down into the linen bag. The action served at least to release some of the tension that had sprung up inside her and gave her time to think. Had she really told him that she was ready to do battle? Surely the means to winning any dispute lay in keeping an element of surprise to confound the enemy? And yet she had inadver-tently given the game away. He must know that she was out to stop him. Had she cooked her goose already? She had the horrible feeling it was well and truly burnt, and he was going to be the man to carve it up.

'Shall we make a start, ladies and gentlemen?' The chairman rose and addressed the assembled crowd. 'I hope that you've had time to calm yourselves and approach this situation in a clearthinking manner. We're all going through difficult times, and I think we all know that none of our problems are going to be easily resolved. Even so…' he turned towards the man who had come to her aid '…I have to say, I believe my colleague, Sam Boyd, is the person who will help us steer our way through choppy waters. Dr Boyd, would you care to address the meeting once more?'

'Thank you, I would.' Sam Boyd stood up and looked confidently around at the sea of faces before him. 'I'm aware of how strongly feelings are running on this issue,' he began, his deep voice flowing over them as smooth as silk. 'I know that the measures we have to put in place will not sit easily with many of you. No one wants to see units closed down and services reduced.'

He let his gaze roam freely, as though he was addressing each person individually, and for a second or two his glance touched on Ruby. Her jaw lifted, letting him know that she would not be sweet-talked. He might have helped her out a short time ago, but this was business, and he was the enemy.

'That's why we're here today,' he went on, 'to discuss the best way to deal with the problem. As you know, the trust is saddled with huge debts, and savings have to be made wherever possible…even at the cost of people's jobs.' He paused momentarily to let that sink in. Then he added, 'This is your chance to put forward your opinions and suggestions. We want to know what you feel about the choices ahead of you.'

The room was silent as the doctors and nurses slowly absorbed what he was saying, and Becky chose that moment to blow a clear and succinct raspberry, followed by a gurgle of excitement as she discovered one of the plastic keys of her teething ring. More raspberries followed.

Sam Boyd appeared to be taken aback for a moment or two. Then his brows rose, and he said on a faintly humorous note,

'Well, that wasn't quite the response I was expecting, but I suppose it's a start, at least.'

A general titter of amusement spread around the room. Embarrassed to be at the centre of attention, Ruby decided that attack was the best form of defence. She stood up and glanced around.

'My apologies for the interruption,' she said. 'I'm Dr Ruby Martyn. As you've probably gathered, I'm having domestic problems at the moment, which means that I have had to bring the baby with me today. I know that on occasion allowances are made for such situations. I do hope that won't be a problem for anybody here, but I was keen to attend this meeting.' She glanced at Becky before adding, 'As you can see, she's not afraid to air her opinions.' She hesitated, allowing time for the audience to settle.

'I have to say, though, I entirely agree with Becky's sentiments on the subject of staff reductions. You cannot remove key personnel and expect things to go on as normal. The doctors and nurses who work here are the lynchpins of this organisation. They are the ones who keep the system going, and reducing numbers will only result in stressed, overworked staff members. The end result will be to bring down morale even further than it has fallen already.'

Sam shook his head. 'The alternative will be to close units down altogether. Is that what you want to see? These debts will not simply fade away. It may be an unpalatable fact, but savings have to be made somehow.'

'And how did those debts come about?' Ruby's grey eyes challenged him. 'I'll remind you, shall I? It was because of the finance deals entered into by the trust board to ensure that the building of the brand new Heritage Hospital could go ahead…the state-of-the-art, be all and end all of hospitals.'

'Yes, that's true.' His tone was appeasing, smoothing over the arguments she'd made as though all was perfectly in order.

'It was a costly venture, I grant you, but many, many lives will be saved because of its existence and because of the up-to-the-minute, high-tech equipment it enjoys.'

'And what of the lives of the people who come here to the Ashvale Hospital, expecting first-rate treatment?' She was warming to her subject, more than ready to tackle him head on. 'How are they going to fare when we're short of doctors and nurses simply because of the measures you're about to take?'

He didn't answer straight away. Instead, he was thoughtful for a moment or two, taking his time in contrast to her quick-fire opposition. 'All right, let's look at that,' he said. 'I can understand perfectly well why you're concerned. But let's take an instance, shall we?' He paused once more, thinking things through. 'Suppose a child is brought here by ambulance, suffering from a severe, life-threatening asthma attack. How many people do you suppose would be involved in his care?'

She thought about that. 'The paramedics, a triage nurse, maybe the senior house officer and a paediatric nurse. There would be a consultant on call to oversee the situation.'

'And between them you expect they would be able to resolve the child's difficulties? They are all essential to the child's well-being?'

'I believe so, yes. Provided that they were able to access him quickly enough and give the right treatment, he should stand a good chance of recovery. That's our job; that's what we're here for, after all. But if there is a breakdown in the chain of personnel brought about by staff shortages, or because people are too busy dealing with other life-threatening emergencies, I can see how things could go drastically wrong.'

He nodded. 'You're right, of course. Having qualified people in place to deal with events as they occur is essential, and no one wants to see staff stretched to the limit, least of all me. But in our hypothetical situation, all the staff and equipment in the world might not have saved the boy…because without the necessary savings to the department, the A&E unit here would have been closed down, and the child would have been transported instead to the Heritage…a journey of a further fifteen miles or so. Given the time taken for that journey, the strong possibility is that he would not have survived.'

There was a combined intake of breath amongst the doctors and nurses in the room as his point sliced home.

Ruby frowned. That was not good. He couldn't be allowed to persuade his audience to submit to his plans by laying out a worst-case scenario as if it were the accepted outcome.

She sent him a direct, lancing stare. 'Do you really think that argument is going to sway me, or anyone here? You're planning to cut the tree off at the roots and afterwards you'll inspect it every now and again to see if it somehow managed to survive.' She shook her head. 'There are other ways to make savings, which don't involve shrinking your prime resource. For instance, you could take a closer look at some of the maintenance and repair contracts that are up for renewal with private companies. You could look to reducing payments for supplies by checking that only essential items are ordered.'

He smiled. It lit up his features, softening his expression and enhancing the perfect angles of his face, and just for an instant, it took her breath away. He was incredibly good-looking, she acknowledged. She hadn't expected to have the rug pulled out from under her in quite that way, and it was a low blow, throwing her out of synch, her nervous system responding with a keen fluttering of sensation, a soft ripple of excitement running along her nerve endings.

'So you want me to cut down on the number of pens I order,' he said, with a soft edge of mockery. 'Well, that's a start, I suppose. And we could talk to the contractors about maintenance and ask them to forego checking the equipment once in a while. I'm not sure how well that would sit with nurses trying to programme a faulty infusion meter, though. It could turn out to be a false economy.'

His answer riled her. 'If you have your way, there might not be a nurse to administer the infusion in the first place,' she retorted, throwing him a cool glance. 'You know as well as I do that commenting on pens and infusion meters is just a cheap jibe. With perseverance, good intent and a willingness to examine all possibilities, we can make this work. There are savings to be made, but we have to choose our targets carefully. I don't believe that units have to be closed, or that staff have to be let go.'

Becky interrupted with an excited babble of baby talk just then, and Ruby glanced down to see that she was shaking her teething rattle with sudden vigour. The tension in the room dissipated as rapidly as it had risen.

'The baby obviously agrees with you,' Sam said, his mouth curving. 'She seems to be a staunch supporter.'

Ruby laughed. 'I'm sure if she was able to speak, she would remind us that people are our greatest asset. We have to work together to make this happen the way we want.'

He nodded and then agreed to take comments from other people in the room. Ruby sat down and tended to Becky, all the while lending an ear to the proceedings. The discussion ebbed and flowed for some time, until eventually the chairman called an end to the meeting.

'We've covered a lot of ground today,' he said. 'Clearly, there has to be a lot more work done before we can decide on our ultimate course, and we welcome suggestions for different strategies from anyone who cares to make them. I suggest we meet again in a few weeks to finalise matters.'

The meeting broke up, and Ruby chatted with James and Olivia for a while, before getting to her feet and preparing to leave the room.

'Dr Martyn...do you have a moment?'

Ruby paused, turning at the sound of Sam Boyd's voice. 'Of course.' She nodded to James and Olivia, and they continued on their way, leaving her free to talk to her new boss.

He studied her thoughtfully for a moment or two. 'I didn't realise, at first, that you're one of the members of my team.'

'Would that have made any difference to our exchange of opinions a while back?'

He shook his head. 'I think you know that it wouldn't. I recognised your name when you introduced yourself. You're my specialist registrar, aren't you?'

She nodded. 'So you've been looking through the personnel files. Perhaps I should give you full marks for staying on the ball.'

He made a mock wince. 'I can see that you believe in being forthright at all times. You're not going to easily accept any changes that I decide to put in place, are you?'

Her expression softened. 'Ah, now there you have it,' she said. 'You see, I do have the interests of the A&E department at heart, and I can promise you that as long as I'm working there I'll do what I can to support my colleagues and steer things in the right direction.'

'As long as you're working there?' He looked at her closely. 'That's an odd turn of phrase. I know your contract's up for renewal at the end of the month, but I assumed you would be staying on. Are you beginning to have doubts about working alongside me? I know that you were a strong contender for the job. Perhaps that's causing you some difficulty?'

She gave his question some thought. 'The board chose you for the post,' she said. 'That was their prerogative, and I accept their decision, although as a follow on from that I'm not altogether sure that you and I will ever see eye to eye. This afternoon has been informative, in more ways than one.'

'That's true,' he murmured. 'It works both ways. And I tend to believe that forewarned is forearmed. I have to respect the way that you spoke your mind back there. I hope you'll go on doing so.'

She gave a short laugh. 'Oh, you can count on it. I usually manage to make my feelings clear, one way or another.'

Becky gurgled, her eyes growing wide as she reached for Ruby, her little arms outstretched, her fists opening and closing in hopeful demand.

'I know, baby,' Ruby said, looking at her. 'You've been cooped up for long enough, haven't you? We'd best get you home.' She glanced back at Dr Boyd and saw that his expression was thoughtful once more. 'I should go now,' she told him.

He frowned. 'Yes, of course. I imagine looking after a baby must take up a great deal of time and energy, and there are all sorts of provisions to be put in place, aren't there? Along with difficulties that occur when things go wrong, such as meetings that crop up and problems with babysitting arrangements.'

'Yes, that's right.'

'I suppose it's understandable that people might have a change of heart when things don't turn out quite as expected.' He glanced at Becky. 'Ambition has its place, but babies can be a job and a half in themselves, can't they?'

She nodded, not quite following his drift. 'I suppose so,' she said. She was all too conscious that Becky was beginning to get restless and she needed to be on her way. She started to walk towards the door. 'I'll say goodbye, then, Dr Boyd.'

He nodded. 'Goodbye. I'll look forward to working with you in A&E…all being well.'

She hurried away from the conference room and whisked Becky out to the car. She wasn't too sure what he had meant by that last turn of phrase…all being well.

It was only when she was halfway home that it occurred to her where Sam Boyd's train of thought must have been heading.

He believed Becky was her child.

CHAPTER TWO

'THERE you are, young Becky,' Ruby said with a smile, 'you're nice and clean and comfortable now, and I expect you're ready for some fun.' She lifted the infant into the air and gently rocked her from side to side, so that she giggled with excitement. 'Exactly…that's just what I meant. You are such a lovely baby.'

She drew her back down and held her close for a moment, enjoying the soft, warm feel of her and breathing in the light fragrance of fresh soap. 'I'll pop you into your bouncer, shall I, so that you can stretch your chubby little legs for a few minutes while I make your tea.'

Ruby had set up the bouncer in the doorway so that she could comfortably watch the child from the kitchen. Once Becky was happily settled, busy touching her toes to the floor and springing up and down within the harness, Ruby set about preparing her food.

It had been a very odd sort of day, so far, many happy moments with Becky interspersed with worry about her sister…and, on top of that, she was still reeling from the effects of coming face to face with her new boss.

How on earth was that going to turn out: working along-side Sam Boyd each day when they were dramatically op-posed to each other's ideas? Added to that, he already had the notion that she resented him for taking the job she had set her heart on, and she had to admit to more than a few niggles on that score.

After all, she'd worked hard to pass her specialist exams and qualify for promotion. Yet what had she actually managed to achieve? These last few years she'd been driven to succeed, spurred on to do her best for the emergency unit where she'd found joy and heartache in equal measure.

It was never going to be an easy option, working in A&E. They faced huge challenges every day, and now the whole department was facing the threat of closure. Did she really want to go through dealing with the stress of that on top of everything else? She was confused, restless, searching for something that she couldn't quite define.

Perhaps the fact that her body clock was ticking away in the background had something to do with the way she was feeling. There was no man in her life any more, not since her relationship with Tom from cardiology had turned sour, and she was less hopeful than ever that there was ever going to be a man who would turn out to be everything she wanted. Maybe he simply didn't exist, or perhaps she was just too cautious.

The trouble was, she had been spoiled by the example of her own extended family. Except for Sophie, who'd had an unfortunate foray into romance with a man who'd left her in the lurch, they were loyal individuals, happy and contented with one another, fulfilled in their relationships. And, as far as Ruby was concerned, no man had ever matched up to the examples she had grown up with.

A few minutes later, as she was spooning hot baby food into a dish, the outer door opened, and Sophie walked into the kitchen. She looked tired, her features pale and drawn.

'Sophie, there you are, at last. I've been so worried about you.' Ruby abandoned the mix of puréed chicken, vegetables and rice that she had been preparing and went to greet her sister. 'What happened to you? I expected you back here ages ago.'

Sophie looked at her anxiously for a moment or two. 'I didn't…' She frowned, trying to get her thoughts together. 'I had to go out…'

'Yes, you did, that's true…to the doctor's surgery, but then you were going to come straight back here, weren't you?'

'Was I?' Sophie frowned, putting a hand to her head as though she was trying to make sense of what was going on. Her dark hair straggled across her cheeks, hiding her face for a moment or two. She reached for a chair and sat down, as though fatigue had overcome her whole body. 'I'm sorry. It's just that I can't seem to think properly these days. I remember there was someone at the surgery…I was worried. I wasn't sure what to do.'

'Someone? The doctor, perhaps?'

Sophie frowned. 'I don't know. I had to get out of there.'

None of this made any sense to Ruby, and Sophie wasn't making things any easier. Giving herself time to think things through, she went to fill the kettle with water at the sink and then set it down on the stovetop to heat. 'I was supposed to go to a meeting. Did you forget about that?'

Sophie's expression was miserable. 'I'm sorry. It must have slipped my mind. I didn't mean to let you down, honestly I didn't.'

From the doorway, Becky became animated, signalling to her mother in eager baby talk that she was there to be noticed, and Sophie turned towards her.

'Oh, baby, you're so beautiful.' Sophie gave her a sweet smile, her heart-shaped features softening as she looked at her daughter. 'I love you to bits, angel. I'm sorry I'm such a bad mother to you.' She glanced at Ruby. 'It's getting late, isn't it? I expect she wants her supper. Shall I give it to her? I see you have it all ready prepared.'

'Are you going to be able to manage it?' Ruby sent her sister a concerned look, worried by the general air of weariness that appeared to have descended on her. 'Maybe if I sit her in the high chair, you could feed her?'

'Yes, I could do that.'

Ruby went over to Becky and released her from the harness, lifting her into the high chair by the table. Judging by Sophie's fragile state, she doubted she would be able to do that safely on her own just now. She drew a clean bib out of a kitchen drawer and handed it to her. 'Here, you'll need this for her. I'll make you a cup of tea, and maybe that will help you to feel a bit better.'

'Thanks, Ruby. You've been so good to me, lately.' Sophie sent her an earnest look. 'I don't know how I would have coped without your help these last few weeks. I've really appreciated being able to stay here with you.' Sophie stopped to cuddle her daughter and plant a kiss on her cheek before fastening the bib carefully around her neck.

Ruby checked the dish of baby food to see if the temperature was cool enough, and then she passed it to Sophie. 'I phoned the surgery, and they told me you hadn't kept your appointment,' she said. 'What happened?'

Sophie frowned. 'I can't remember. I think I felt sick and had to go out for some air. I'm not too sure what happened after that. I just started to walk and kept on walking.'

Ruby studied her for a moment or two. 'You haven't been sleeping very well, lately, have you? Perhaps you'll feel better after you've had some rest. Then, when you're up to it, we really need to take you back to the surgery so that the doctor can find out what's wrong. You can't go on like this.'

She had the feeling, though, that Sophie was no longer listening to her. Looking over, she saw she was gently coaxing Becky to eat the food, making soft, encouraging noises, as though she was savouring the meal herself.

Ruby sighed inwardly. How were the pair of them going to cope when she wasn't there to watch over them? She thought briefly about taking a day or two off work, but the image of Sam Boyd crept into her mind, and she imagined those dark brows lifting as he contemplated her lax attitude. She'd been late for the meeting, and if she added time off to that lapse, he would surely have her marked down as unreliable. No, she had to face him on equal terms. It was a matter of pride.

Perhaps she could persuade the next-door neighbour to keep an eye on Sophie and Becky while she went out to work tomorrow? Claire had turned out to be a good friend who was usually glad to help in any way she could.

Either way, it was a worrying situation that had been building up for some time, and it had to be sorted out once and for all. She made up her mind that next time she would go along with her sister to the surgery. That way she could make sure that things went according to plan.

'Do you think you might be happier going to stay with Mum and Dad for a while?' she asked, coming to sit down at the table and beginning to pour tea. 'I think you need someone to look after you properly until you're feeling better.'

'Oh, I don't think that would work out very well,' Sophie said, shaking her head. 'Mum and Dad are way too busy. Mum has her job at the office, and Dad has to concentrate on pulling the business into shape. Besides, don't you remember—they asked me if I would look after the smallholding while Gran and Grandad are away for the next few weeks. I said I would do it…only it would be so much better if you were there with me, and there's plenty of room at the old farmhouse. I'm not sure I could handle things very well on my own, though. I don't seem able to think too clearly these days.'

Ruby nodded. 'I remember.' The trouble was, Sophie was probably right in thinking she wouldn't be able to cope, and Ruby didn't have an easy solution to hand.

Sophie was dejected. 'I know this place is too small for all of us. I don't mean to be a burden.'

Ruby frowned. 'I wasn't suggesting that I didn't want you here with me. That wasn't what I meant at all. I love having you and Becky here…you must know that. It's just that I think you're unwell and you need more help than I can give you while I'm working. Of course I'll come along and stay with you at the old farmhouse, but I don't think you're in any state to be left there on your own while I'm out at the hospital.'

Maybe she could make arrangements for someone to keep an eye on her at the smallholding. The local vet, perhaps? He was more of a friend to the family than a professional that they looked to for help on occasion. Ruby and Sophie had even been at school with him. He had his practice close by her grandparents home, and his work often brought him to the farm, where he would check up on the animals.

Sophie didn't acknowledge any of what she was saying. She seemed depressed, her shoulders slumping as though she was weighed down by an ominous black cloud.

'I'll play with Becky for a while, and then I'll take her upstairs and get her settled down for bed,' Sophie said a few minutes later as she wiped her daughter's face clean. 'After that, I think I'll have an early night. I'm very tired.'

'That's a good idea, but maybe you should have something to eat first. I made a salad, and there's crusty bread and cheese to go with it.'

'Okay.'

They ate together in the kitchen, and Sophie perked up enough to ask Ruby about her job at the hospital. 'You have a new boss taking over from the man who's retiring, don't you? Have you met him yet? Do you think things are going to work out for you in A&E with him in charge?'

Ruby's mouth made a wry twist. 'I met him today, and he seems to be very determined to push through the changes he has in mind, even though they're not at all popular. I'm not sure how it's all going to work out. I expect life in the A&E department is going to be quite rocky from here on.'

A short time later, Sophie helped to clear away the supper dishes and then took Becky upstairs to bathe her and settle her for the night. Ruby went to check on them from time to time to make sure that all was going smoothly, but Sophie seemed to be coping well enough. Once she and the baby were both tucked up in their beds and fast asleep, she slipped next door to ask if Claire would keep an eye on them the following day.

'I'll find an excuse to keep popping round,' Claire said. She was a friendly woman in her early forties, with teenage daughters who simply adored Becky. 'Don't you worry. Everything will be fine.'

It was a relief to know that they would be in good hands, and Ruby set out for work next day feeling a little more reassured. She would be able to concentrate on the job in hand, and her biggest worry was whether things would run smoothly in A&E now that Dr Stanford had retired and the new boss was taking his place. With any luck, it would be a seamless transfer.

All was not well, though, she discovered. When she walked into the emergency unit later that morning, after spending some time reviewing patients' progress in the observation ward, she found that there was a general air of discontent about the place.

'Okay, so what's the matter with everyone?' Ruby asked, taking a quick look around the resuscitation area and then inspecting the assembled crowd in the waiting room. 'There are far too many long faces around here.'

'I think you've just seen for yourself,' James murmured. He drew a chart from the pile on the desk and cast a quick glance over the notes. 'It's still relatively early in the day, and we're already stretched tight at the seams.'

'We've had five people brought in by ambulance from

rush-hour traffic accidents,' Olivia added, going over to the whiteboard and writing up more names. 'And the waiting room is heaving with an assortment of fractures, sprains, nasty infections and people with chest pains.'

'Sounds like everything's perfectly normal, then,' Ruby said with a laugh. 'It's a case of heads down and let's get on with it, to my way of thinking.'

'Hah! You'd think so, wouldn't you?' James's mouth made a downward turn. 'Except that two of the nurses are off sick, one of the doctors has gone home to deal with a domestic crisis, and we have no one to replace them.'

Ruby raised her brows. 'No agency nurses or a locum doctor?'

'None,' he answered. 'Not a one.'

'Hmm. That certainly is going to make life difficult.'

'Apparently we're banned from bringing them in on account of it being too costly, and all overtime beyond a certain level has been stopped.' James's tone was edged with annoyance.

'I almost paged you at one stage, but Dr Boyd said you were dealing with an emergency in the observation ward and we'd cope.' Olivia pulled a face. 'I suppose he was right, and we did manage, but we're run off our feet, and patients are already complaining about waiting times.'

'I guess Dr Boyd is behind the restriction on agency staff,' Ruby mused. So he had kept tabs on her while she was working in the observation ward, had he? He obviously had his finger on the pulse of how the department ran, but she could certainly see why the two doctors were feeling under pressure. 'He didn't waste any time putting his plans into action, did he? He must be very keen to pull the department into shape.'

'That's right. I'm the one who put a stop to the extra staff. It costs way too much to bring in staff from outside.' A now familiar voice came from behind her, and she swivelled around to see the man himself standing just a couple of feet away. Ruby studied him briefly. He was immaculately dressed, as before, in a dark grey suit and crisply laundered shirt, with a silk tie that was perfect in its understated elegance. 'What do we have here,' he asked, 'a union meeting?'

'Dr Boyd,' Ruby acknowledged him. 'It's good to see you again…albeit in difficult circumstances.'

'Call me Sam,' he said in a brisk tone. 'No need to stand on ceremony.' He frowned. 'As to the circumstances, you should all know from the outset that I don't believe in letting the grass grow under my feet. It's important to start as we mean to go on if we're to have any chance at all of saving the A&E unit. We're not playing at this. It isn't a game. It's for real.'

'I know. I'm sure we're all aware of that.' Ruby made a muted response to his bracing tone. Perhaps he was annoyed because they had been talking about him, and they needed to make allowances for that. She added softly, 'And I expect the problems that follow will be for real, too. I'll leave you to deal with the complaints from the patients, shall I, and from the management when we fail to meet targets?'

He acknowledged that with a rueful twist of his mouth. 'I imagine those will be the least of my worries.' He gave her an assessing glance, his gaze shimmering downwards over her curves outlined by the soft cotton blouse that clung where it touched and then draped itself loosely over the waistband of her calf-length skirt. 'Besides, I'm sure I can rely on you to help smooth things over during these difficult times. I hear you're good at dealing with most problems that come your way. You appear to have a knack for calming troubled waters. Perhaps that's why the department operated so efficiently while Dr Stanford was winding down for his retirement.'

Ruby's eyes widened a fraction. Where would he have gleaned that wedge of information? Was it possible that he had been talking to his predecessor? Or maybe one or two of the board members had filled him in on her way of working. They might not have given her the job, but it didn't necessarily mean they were unaware of her capabilities. Her lips made a wry shape. Perhaps her calm attitude was what had lost her the position. They wanted a lion that would roar and show its teeth.

Sam glanced at James and Olivia. 'I know this is difficult for all of you, but there's no point in moping about the situation. What we have to do is prioritise, knuckle down and get on with the job and concentrate on providing the best service we can under the circumstances.'

He turned to James and held out a patient's file to him, his manner totally businesslike. 'You examined a man who came in earlier with a broken wrist and suspected head injury after a fall…is that right?'

James nodded. 'Tony Barton…a young man in his late twenties. I treated him for the wrist fracture and assessed him for brain injury, but his neurological responses were fine. I was getting ready to discharge him.' He glanced at the file. 'Are you ready to sign off his notes for me?'

Sam shook his head. 'His condition has changed, according to the nurse who was following up on him. I'd like you to come with me and take another look at him, please.'

'Oh…of course.' James's colour faded, and Ruby could see that he was wondering if he was in trouble of some sort. He was usually thorough and conscientious in everything that he did, but Sam, being a newcomer, clearly didn't know that.

Sam nodded towards Ruby and Olivia and then strode off with James in the direction of the treatment room.

Ruby's gaze met Olivia's, and the senior house officer rolled her eyes. 'Does that man ever stop to engage in the niceties of getting to know his colleagues?' Olivia asked. 'He's brisk and businesslike, and his whole attitude is "stop fussing and let's get on with it", though I must say he seems half inclined to pass the time of day with you…but as to the rest of us…' Olivia sucked in a deep breath. 'He's only been here five minutes, and I'm already beginning to wish Dr Stanford had delayed his retirement.'

Ruby grinned. 'I dare say we'll get used to him, given time. He has a huge task ahead of him, and he's probably still working on his strategies. I expect he has a heart of gold underneath it all.'

'We'll have to dig deep to find it,' Olivia murmured, moving away in search of her next patient. 'I have the feeling it's buried under a ton of steel.'

She could be right in that. Ruby frowned as she riffled through the files in the wire tray. Their new boss didn't appear to be making any concessions to the fact that he was a stranger in their midst, and that they might have difficulty getting used to this different way of working. It was all or nothing with him.

She glanced through the list of patients waiting to be seen. Her first job was to check on the patients from the traffic accident, and in doing that her time was taken up with a host of complications that had arisen from an assortment of broken bones and punctured blood vessels. Worryingly, one man went into cardiac arrest, and she had to use the defibrillator to shock his heart back into a safe rhythm.

'He's back with us,' she said a few minutes later, addressing the nurse who was monitoring his situation. 'Give the intensive care unit another call, will you, and see if we can move him over there as soon as possible.'

'I'll do that,' the nurse said.

An hour later things settled down a little, giving her time to attend to a young boy who had been injured during a football match on his local playing field.

'That was an unlucky game for you, Matt, from the sound of things,' she said, smiling at the seven-year-old and then inspecting the X-ray film displayed in the light box. 'When you fell to the ground, you hit it with enough force to break your collarbone. That's this one, here.' She pointed out the area of the fracture to the boy and his mother. 'There's a line across here that shows the break in the bone.'

She turned to look at Matt once more. 'The good news is, it should heal up quite well because the two pieces of bone are still in line and touching one another. You'll need to wear a support sling for a week or two while the bone heals, and we'll give you some painkillers to help you feel better.'

His mouth made a flat line. 'If I'd done this in a couple of weeks' time, when school starts again, I could have had some days off. And I don't even get a plaster cast for my friends to sign.' He looked thoroughly disgruntled.

'Isn't there any street cred in wearing a sling?' Ruby lifted a brow. 'I would have thought you could get some pretty good mileage out of that. And it's the hand that you write with that's out of action, isn't it? I'll bet you can impress your mates with a left-handed signature.'

His expression brightened. 'Yeah, maybe.'

His mother smiled as they stood up to leave a few minutes later. 'I'm sure he'll milk this for all it's worth,' she murmured in an undertone to Ruby. 'He'll be playing the part of a wounded secret agent before too long, I'll be bound.'

Ruby nodded agreement, and gave Matt a bravery certificate as he left the room. It seemed he was already working on his game plan. 'Tyler didn't get one of these when he sprained his ankle,' he said. 'He only got a badge that was this big.' His fingers made demonstration of its tiny size.

Ruby laughed and watched them leave before going in search of her next patient. She worked steadily through the morning, dealing with a wide variety of injuries suffered by active young children intent on enjoying their summer holidays to the full, while at the same time keeping an eye on the work of the senior house officers in her charge. Sam was nowhere to be seen.

James had been missing for some time, too, but she caught sight of him when she was heading towards the ambulance bay. An infant with breathing difficulties was being brought in to A&E by ambulance, and she expected him to arrive in the next few minutes.

'Is everything all right, James?' she asked now, still continuing on her way. 'You look as though you're in shock.'

James fell into step beside her. 'I'm fine,' he said. 'I just don't know how my patient could have gone downhill so rapidly. One minute he was sitting there, talking to us, and the next his speech started to slur, and he began to sink into unconsciousness. And to think I almost sent him home.'

'What happened?'

'Sam—Dr Boyd—did a CT scan and then whisked him up to the operating theatre. He told me to scrub in. It turns out that he specialised as a neurosurgeon originally and then after several years of doing that decided to take up emergency medicine.' He shook his head in wonder. 'Everything happened so fast. It seemed like within minutes the anaesthetist was there and the patient was out for the count, and then Sam was cutting a segment out of his skull.'

'So it was a blood clot causing pressure on the brain?'

James nodded. 'That's right. I actually got to suction it out, but then Sam took over and stopped the bleeding. He says we have to watch him for swelling on the brain and seizures, and I have to keep an eye on him. I'm just on my way to talk to the man's wife. She came in to the hospital expecting to take him home, but now, of course, he'll be admitted to the surgical ward.'

Ruby glanced at James. 'You sound as though the experience has opened your eyes in some way. I don't think I've ever seen you quite so shaken up.'

He nodded. 'Well, he's not out of the woods yet, and that's a worry, but thinking about what might have happened, and seeing our new boss at work, has given me something to think about. Not only that, but it's made me wonder if I ought to consider going in for a surgical specialty after my stint here. Watching him operate really made me see how much of a difference a surgeon can make to someone's chances of recovery.'

'Then something good has come out of this. I'm pleased for you, James.'

He made a brief smile and went on his way, while Ruby hurried to the ambulance bay, deep in thought. So Sam was more than just a force to be reckoned with on the hospital administration side of things. He was a first-rate doctor as well. It was more or less what she had expected, but somehow she had thought it might take more time for him to prove himself. At least he had managed to win James over to his side, brisk manner notwithstanding.

She went to meet the paramedics a short time later as they wheeled the infant out of the ambulance on a trolley bed.

'This is Charlie, eighteen months old,' the paramedic said. 'He's struggling to breathe, and there's some nasal flaring. His blood oxygen level is low, and he's in severe distress.'

Ruby could see at once that Charlie was very ill and the muscles of his rib cage were sucking inwards. 'Let's get him into the treatment room,' she said. The toddler was breathing in oxygen through a mask, but she could hear him wheezing, and it was clear he needed urgent help.

Once in the treatment room, she called for a nurse to assist with giving oxygen while she examined the boy. Running the stethoscope over his chest, she heard crackles in his lungs and a wheeze whenever he breathed out.

His mother looked on anxiously the whole time, and after a while Ruby said, 'He's feverish and obviously struggling. I believe his air passages could be inflamed, so we'll try him with a medication to help ease his breathing.'

'What's wrong with him?' his mother asked. 'He's had a runny nose for a few days now, but suddenly he seemed to go downhill, breathing fast and getting tired and irritable. He's been off his food too.'

'It's probably a viral infection of some sort,' Ruby explained. 'I'll do a nasal swab and send it to the lab to be sure what we're dealing with, but in the meantime we'll concentrate on supporting his breathing. We'll keep him in our observation ward for the next twenty-four hours, and then we'll most likely have to move him to the paediatric ward for a few days. The nurse will explain everything to you and make arrangements for you to stay with him if that's what you want to do.'

'Yes, I do. Thank you.' The young woman leaned over and stroked her child's hand, offering him comfort, but the boy was too ill to respond. He just lay there, unmoving, strands of his hair curling damply over his forehead.

'Here, take a seat,' the nurse said, pulling a chair to one side of the bed. Michelle was a capable girl, slender and pretty, with dark hair that fell in a sleek bob to the nape of her neck. 'I'm sure he knows that you're here with him, and that will help to ease his distress.'

Ruby knew that she was leaving the mother and child in good hands. She wrote up the boy's chart, detailing the medication to be given, and then arranged for the nasal swab to be sent to the lab. 'I'll look in on Charlie again soon,' she told the mother, knowing that the nurse would let her know if any problem came up in the meantime.

'So there you are,' Sam greeted her as she walked back into the main area of A&E. 'I'm afraid we have to prepare for another intake of crash victims. There are expected to be around ten of them, according to the paramedics at the scene. The first will be arriving in about fifteen minutes, they say.' He shook his head. 'I can't imagine what's happening out there on the roads today.'

'People are travelling to the coast for holidays, or driving back home,' she guessed. 'I suppose that means there's a lot more traffic out there.'

'Maybe.' He paused. 'Before we get ourselves immersed in the chaos of dealing with the intake and I lose sight of you again for the next hour or so, I wanted to ask if you know anything about what the situation is here with the domestic staff. We don't seem to have a proper clean-up crew—to attend to mishaps and the like in the waiting room. There just seems to be a couple of ward assistants who bring round the coffee, or tend to the book trolley, and descend on the unit if and when they're called for. I've been asking various people, but no one seems to want to give me a proper answer.'

'Hmm.' Her brow knotted. 'I believe you're talking about Dolly and Mabel. Don't you go upsetting either of them. They're our in-house treasures. We rely on them for all sorts of odd jobs, and I don't think people would take kindly to you striking them off the staff list.'

'No, probably not.' He studied her thoughtfully. 'You're frowning,' he said. 'I have the strong feeling that it's because of me, or something I've said. I've been getting a lot of that today. Would you care to enlighten me?'

'Well, I know the situation here is serious,' she murmured. 'Times are hard, and we all have to pull together to get the job done and all that…but I think you really need to try and loosen up a bit.' She hesitated, not wanting to go too far. He was the one in charge, after all.

'I do?'

She shrugged her shoulders, giving in to his gentle prompting. What would it matter if she were the one to tell him a few home truths? No one else would consider doing it. 'Quite definitely. We really shouldn't lose sight of the human touch, you know. We aren't in the boardroom now, and even the most difficult of tasks can be made sweeter with a modicum of pleasantry.'

He raised a dark brow. 'You're saying you think I'm too abrupt?'

She made a vacillating kind of movement, as though she was weighing things in the balance. 'I'm afraid you run the risk of alienating the people you depend on,' she said.

He made a face. 'I dare say you're the one to put me right on that score. From what I've gathered this morning, I'm sure you'll be well able to assist me in pulling things into shape. You're the one topic people are prepared to talk about. I've been hearing nothing but glowing accounts of your capabilities in this department.'

'I'm sorry about that,' she said with a laugh. 'You sound as though it's beginning to grate on your nerves.'

'Not at all. It's good to know that we have such a diamond in our midst. I'll be glad of all the help I can get.'

'We've always been a happy crowd here at Ashvale A&E.' She didn't add, before he came along, but he probably caught her meaning.

'I guess I've a lot to learn.' It didn't seem to bother him, though. He glanced at the watch on his wrist. 'Anyway, back to the immediate problem. I've asked Michelle to do triage, the senior house officers will take the urgent cases, and you and I will deal with the most seriously injured. It means we'll be running at full tilt with a minimum of staff.'

He checked the whiteboard, assessing the number of patients still in attendance and needing to be seen. 'I'll have a word with the nursing sister on duty and see if we can have some of her specialists attend to the less serious cases in the waiting room. That should clear the backlog.'

He glanced at her as though looking for confirmation, and she raised a brow. 'Are you asking if I agree? I told you, if you were trying to save money, I think you should have looked to cutting down on the maintenance contracts before you went ahead and dispensed with nursing services. We don't need to have the light bulbs checked once a month, or have laundry sent to an outside company when we have perfectly adequate facilities on the premises. Nor do we need to order paper plates on a regular basis when we have dishwashers and crockery on site.'

His mouth made a crooked shape. 'I wasn't looking for a debate on the whys and wherefores. A simple "yes, that sounds about right" would have done.' His eyes took on a glimmer of amusement. 'I was attempting to keep you in the loop, so to speak, since it's fairly obvious you're the lynchpin around here. Is there anything else you think we need to have in place?'

She thought about it. 'Yes,' she murmured after a second or two. 'We need doughnuts.'

'I beg your pardon?' He looked at her as though for a moment she'd lost the plot.

'You won't get by without them,' she said on a firm note. 'If you expect your staff to work through their lunch breaks and keep going without flagging, you'll have to do something to boost their energy as well as their morale.' She gave him a bright smile. 'I've always found that doughnuts hit the spot. Mark my words. A little bit of sugar goes a long way.'

'I'll try to remember that,' he said. He threw her a teasing look as his gaze wandered over her softly feminine curves. 'You're not on any kind of diet, are you? So if I were to feed you sugary sweet doughy treats, would that help to bring you on side? I could rely on you to be my right-hand woman?'

She sent him a direct grey glance. 'I certainly won't say no to the food…but as for any other outlandish expectations you might be harbouring, I wouldn't push your luck, if I were you. I'm only ever on the side that looks to be about right.'

He tilted his head back in a resigned gesture. 'I might have known,' he murmured. His mouth curved. 'Still, it was worth a try.'

CHAPTER THREE

'IT'S really good of you to help me out like this.' Ruby thanked the woman who was running the crèche at the hospital. 'I don't know what I would have done if you hadn't been able to find a place for Becky at such short notice.'

'Well, you did say it was just for a few days, and we have a couple of vacant places available while people are away on holiday.' The woman smiled, watching Becky as she lay gurgling on the mat, trying to clasp the plastic toys that dangled overhead from the play gym. 'She looks as though she's a contented child.'

'Yes, she is, for the most part.' Which was just as well, because with all the problems that had cropped up of late, Ruby was sure she wouldn't have been able to cope with a fractious infant. Things had been going reasonably well until the day before yesterday, when Sophie had gone out, saying she was going on an errand to the shops. When she didn't return, Ruby had begun to worry.

There was still no sign of her, and Ruby was becoming increasingly anxious. She had tried contacting her by phone, and she'd searched high and low before frantically enlisting the help of the police. Sophie was now officially a missing person, and no one had any idea where she had gone.

It had all come as such a shock, and now Ruby was finding

it difficult to juggle work in A&E with looking after the baby. How was she going to cope when she had to move into the farmhouse over the weekend now that Sophie was gone? There would be a whole lot more problems for her to concentrate on then.

'I'll come back at lunchtime to see how she's getting on,' she said, reluctantly preparing to leave.

'That's good.' The nursery matron gave Ruby a reassuring smile, probably sensing her underlying anxiety. 'I'm sure she'll be fine.'

Yes, most likely she would. Ruby cast a last, fleeting glance at the baby before she left the room. Becky had no idea of the disturbance that had ebbed and flowed around her since her mother's health had begun to decline. And now Sophie was missing.

Bracing herself to face the rest of the day, Ruby made her way back down to A&E. She stopped by the central desk and made a few phone calls, first of all, checking up on the patients who had spent the previous day in the observation ward.

'No problems to speak of,' Lorraine, the nursing supervisor, told her. 'We've arranged for two children with chest infections, query pneumonia, to be admitted, as you asked. Apart from those, everyone else looks fit enough to be discharged.'

'That's good to hear. I'll drop by later this morning and finish the paperwork.' Ruby hesitated. 'Is there any news on Charlie—the infant with breathing difficulties? I put him on humidified oxygen, and then we had to add nebulised adrenaline because he wasn't responding too well to treatment. Last time I went to see him he was showing a little bit of improvement.'

'The boy with bronchiolitis? Yes, I checked for you. He was admitted to the paediatric ward from Intensive Care, and by all accounts he's doing fine.'

'Oh, that's brilliant. Thanks for checking for me, Lorraine.'

'You're very welcome. See you later, then.'

'Yes, I'll come over to you in a couple of hours or so.' Ruby replaced the receiver and began to hunt through a pile of papers in the wire tray on the desk.

'Nothing's going according to plan lately,' Olivia said, coming to stand beside her. 'I thought things were bad enough when I heard that we have two nurses off sick, but then I saw the management circular that was passed around first thing this morning. They're talking about downgrading us to an urgent care centre…and that's even before the meeting where it's all supposed to be decided.' She huffed, showing her annoyance.

'I don't know how our trauma victims would have fared if they'd been sent to the Heritage,' Ruby commented. 'Some of them were in a precarious condition when they arrived here.' As it was, the patients who had been involved in traffic accidents a few days ago had either been operated on and were now recovering on the wards, or had been discharged.

Ruby glanced at the senior house officer briefly. Olivia was in a decidedly crotchety mood today, her usually serene face etched with lines of tension. 'Is that all that's bothering you?'

'Not really. I took a look in the waiting room, and straight-away I wished I hadn't.'

'Oh, why's that?' Ruby glanced through a sheaf of lab test results, searching for a diagnosis on a small patient. If only her sister Sophie's medical problems could have been properly diagnosed before she'd decided to take off. For that must be what lay behind her disappearance, surely? She didn't think anything more sinister lay behind her failure to return, given that the police had let her know that she had been spotted boarding a bus in town on the day she had vanished without a trace.

Olivia started to answer, and Ruby dragged her mind back to the job in hand.

'I'm out of sorts because that man's in there again…the one who's kept complaining of back pain ever since he was involved in a car accident some time ago. He's been in here several times over the last few months, but we never seem to be able to get to the bottom of what's causing his problems. Dr Stanford said they'd done all the tests and found no lasting damage. He told him he should go and see his GP about any symptoms he has, but he always comes up with some reason why he has to be here in emergency. Today it's because he almost passed out when he went to fetch something from the local garage, and the manager brought him straight to the hospital.'

'Oh, I see.' Ruby nodded. 'Well, I'll take a look at him if you like. We're not exactly overrun with dire emergencies at the moment, are we?' She clamped a hand over her mouth. 'Oh, I can't believe I just said that.'

'Said what? Is there a problem?' Sam came to join them at the desk, tilting his head slightly to one side as he cast a quizzical glance over her. His black hair was crisply styled, framing his strong-boned features to perfection. His blue-grey eyes studied her curiously. 'You've not been your usual self these last few days, have you? Is something wrong?'

Ruby gazed at him in wonder, slightly thrown by his tall, dark presence. She ought to be used by now to the way he had of appearing out of nowhere, but perhaps she wasn't fully on the ball. Somehow or other he always managed to make her heart leap into an odd, hasty rhythm.

As to her mood, she was startled that he had even noticed her frame of mind. He was always so busy tending to seriously ill patients or organising the day-to-day management of the unit. Because of the cutbacks he had been forced to make, there were new difficulties arising all the time.

She shook her head. 'Nothing's wrong. Everything's fine.' She wasn't going to lay out all her troubles for him to pick over. He was a man, first of all, energetic, efficient and direct, everything appearing clearly black or white, and he would probably have next to no understanding of the emotional side of things, the grey edges that tended to blur judgement.

'Except that she just said how quiet it is in here today,' Olivia pointed out. 'You know what that means, don't you? Lights will start flashing and sirens will be blaring within seconds, and the next thing you know, we'll be swamped under a deluge of patients.' She shook her head. 'Even I know not to tempt fate that way.' Her mouth made a flat line. 'Still, we have to make allowances, I suppose. Ruby has to go and take over at her Gran's smallholding this weekend, so she's probably not thinking straight. Just contemplating the work involved would be enough to make me quake. Cleaning out the chicken run…mucking out after the ponies…and that's before we even get to the goats.'

'Goats? Good grief.' Sam's brows shot up. 'You're not seriously going to do all that, are you?' he asked, looking at Ruby.

'For a few weeks, yes,' she told him. 'My grandparents are going away for a while, and they've asked the family to help. There's no one else who can sort it out for us. Not without it costing us a small fortune, anyway.'

She contemplated the prospect of living in the Chilterns for the next few weeks and gave a soft sigh. Perhaps it was just what she needed right now—a complete change. Time to be with Becky and attempt to smooth over the unhappy disappearance of her mother that had shaken the baby's world. Life was incredibly hard for her just now. She was juggling too many things all at once: coming to terms with the fact that Sophie had gone away, learning how to cope with looking after Becky on her own…and trying to accept that she had lost the job she wanted to a man who had swept in on a wave of budget-cutting zeal. Add to that the fact that her grandparents needed her help, and the mix was well and truly bubbling, threatening to boil over.

She frowned. 'Actually, I think it might be just the thing for me…I still haven't taken all of my annual leave this year, and there's a certain appeal to sampling fresh country air and taking a break from all the frantic activity that goes on around here.'

She remained perfectly still for a while, mulling things over. The more she thought about it, the more the option of leaving her job altogether appealed.

'Now, there's a thought…my contract comes to an end in a fortnight's time, doesn't it? And I don't necessarily have to renew it since I haven't signed on the dotted line yet.' Somehow, she hadn't been able to bring herself to put in the necessary paperwork. 'I do earn some income from the medical articles I write for magazines and so on. And there's the online medical forum, as well—they pay me a retainer for doing that.'

It would be a difficult choice to make—after all, she needed money if she was to look after Becky—but the prospect of turning her back on the whirlwind of her career and leaving it to Sam to take up where she left off was becoming more interesting by the minute. He wanted the job—he had been given it at her expense—maybe he should be left to deal with it in its entirety.

'You're joking, aren't you?' Sam was frowning, looking at her intently as though he would like to be able to read her mind.

'About the online forum? No.' She shook her head. 'We answer questions from people who have worries about their various symptoms or illnesses, or who want a little more detail than their GP is able to give them.'

'I meant about leaving here.' His voice was terse.

Ruby mused on that for a while. 'I'm not altogether sure. In fact, the more I think about it, the more tempting it becomes.' After all, what prospects were there for her here? With the possibility of the unit being downgraded, things were beginning to look quite bleak, one way or another. Sam would be all right whatever happened because he worked from both hospital sites—the Ashvale and the Heritage. And the SHOs would find placements at other hospitals. It was the patients and the people who lived in the local area who would lose out most of all because of the effects of the closure.

She picked up the chart outlining the symptoms of the man who suffered from the painful back and the recent fainting spell. 'I have to go,' she said. 'Just in case I have brought us bad luck, and we're about to be inundated.'

Sam was still frowning as she walked away, but Ruby needed some space. Life was difficult, she was worried about her sister, and now she unexpectedly had a baby to care for. None of her problems was going to be easily resolved.

'Mr Dryden—Nick,' she greeted the patient as she walked into the treatment room. He was lying on a trolley bed, propped up by pillows. 'May I call you by your first name?'

He nodded. 'That's fine.'

'Good.' She looked him over briefly before glancing at the notes on the chart. He looked vaguely familiar to her, and now she realised it was probably because he had attended the department on several occasions. He was lean, thin faced with pale features, his brown hair slightly dishevelled, and he appeared to be restless.

'You say that you've been feeling a bit woozy,' she said after a moment or two.

'Yeah. I was at the local garage, trying to buy a spare part for my car, and my legs buckled under me. The manager gave me a lift here.'

'I see. Do you have pain anywhere in particular?'

'Nowhere specially just now—except my back's always playing me up. Gives me quite a bit of gyp. I was a passenger in a car that was rear ended a couple of years ago.'

Ruby nodded. 'I see you're taking pain medication. You're on quite a high dose of narcotic pain relief, aren't you?'

He sent her a quick, challenging look. 'You're not going

to try to take that away from me, are you? If anything, I need a stronger prescription. You want to try living in constant pain.' He frowned. 'Well, you probably don't, but take my word for it, it sucks.'

'I wasn't going to suggest anything of the sort,' she murmured. 'Although there are probably other medications that would be better for you—anti-inflammatories, for a start.'

He shook his head. 'I'd prefer to stick to what I have. We've tried all the other stuff before.'

'Hmm.' Ruby was thoughtful for a while. Something about this man bothered her. He didn't look quite right, and her instinct was telling her that his problems needed more investigation.

'According to these notes, your blood pressure was low when the nurse took a reading earlier,' she said. 'I think I'll check it again, and then I'd like to do a blood test to see if there's an imbalance in your blood chemistry. You're very pale, so it's possible that you're a bit anaemic. That can sometimes be a cause of dizzy spells.'

'Sure, go ahead.' He seemed perfectly relaxed about it, and it was Ruby's feeling that he wasn't in too much discomfort right then.

Even so, she had the idea that something about his condition didn't quite add up, and so she went ahead and completed both procedures. His blood pressure was slightly lower than before, and his pulse was a little faster, but that was probably because he was here in the hospital being asked to answer questions.

'I'll leave you to rest for a while,' she said. 'As soon as we have the results of the blood test, I'll come back and see you.'

'Okay.' He nodded and leaned back against his pillows.

She left him and went to see to her other patients. A young girl had suffered a badly sprained ankle, and she spent some time looking at the X-rays and examining her before arranging for it to be supported in a temporary cast. 'I'll give you some medicine to take away the pain,' she told the girl. 'You need to keep your weight off it for a few days.'

Turning to the girl's mother, she said, 'I'd like you to bring her in to our orthopaedic department in a week's time so that the specialist can take a look at her. In the meantime, I'll give you a letter to pass on to your GP.'

'Thanks.'

The morning passed swiftly, and Ruby caught sight of Sam from time to time as he dealt with the more seriously injured people who were brought in. She knew from helping Dr Stanford to run the department that he had a lot to contend with. His time was taken up with everything from treating trauma victims, and giving lectures to eager young medical students, to arranging for faulty equipment to be serviced. He was a very busy man.

He didn't usually stop to chat with his fellow workers for very long in between attending to his patients, which meant that they tended to view him as someone who stood apart from them.

Ruby frowned, thinking about that. Was he ever bothered by a sense of isolation from his colleagues? It was all very well for him to decide that he was an independent soul who didn't need anyone, but that way of going on could lead to disaster; no man was an island. Maybe she should do whatever was possible to try to save him from himself.

'Do you need any help?' she asked when she saw him attempting to deal with an infant who was crying inconsolably. The child was lying in his mother's lap, and Ruby guessed he was about a year old. He was pulling up his legs and screaming as though he was in pain. 'I guess we have no nurses to spare at the moment. They're all busy helping out with orthopaedic problems and lacerations.'

He gave her a harassed look as though bringing up the subject of staff shortages was a low blow. 'Thanks. If you're not embroiled in anything, I really need to examine this little fellow, but he absolutely doesn't want me to do that.' He glanced at the child's mother, who gave him an apologetic look in return.

'He's been like this for a while,' the young woman said softly. 'It's as though he gets a cramping pain and doubles up. He's been vomiting, as well.'

Sam nodded. 'His tummy is swollen too, but I don't think I'm going to get a chance to have a proper look at that.'

'I could try distracting him,' Ruby said, going to rummage in a nearby cupboard. 'Wait till the cramping pain goes away and he settles a bit, and then I'll show him our teddy bear while you do your bit.'

He smiled. 'Sounds like a good idea to me.'

'It usually does the trick,' she said, bringing out an assortment of toys in a plastic tray. 'If it doesn't, we'll try a musical diversion…as long as the battery's working.' She pressed a button on a small box connected to a miniature carousel, and the strains of a lullaby filled the room.

The baby stopped crying and instead began to make small sobbing sounds as he turned his head to see where the tinkling music was coming from. Then he reached out a hand as if he wanted to grab this fascinating new toy. Ruby unhooked one of the plastic horses from the carousel and gave it to him.

Between them they managed to divert his attention long enough for Sam to complete the examination. He was gentle but thorough and, above all, swift. As she watched him with the baby, Ruby felt an unfamiliar knot come into her throat. He was such a strong, focussed man, yet with this infant he was tender, caring, unwilling to add in any way to his pain. All the time he was examining him, he was conscious of the boy's responses, and he spoke to him in a soft, soothing voice.

He was thoughtful for a while afterwards, reading through the notes on the child's history, and then he told the mother, 'I want to do some further investigations, Mrs Franklyn—an ultrasound scan, first of all, and then maybe a CT scan after he's had a drink of something that will show up on the images.'

'Is it serious, then?' The woman looked worried.

'We don't know anything for sure right now,' he said softly. 'Let's do the tests and see if we can find out what's going on. Either way, I promise you we'll take good care of him.'

'Thanks.'

A few minutes later, they left the room, leaving the woman to sit with her child and take his mind off his discomfort with the toys.

Ruby asked, 'Are you thinking it's some kind of obstruction to the intestine?'

'Maybe. It could be a twisting of the intestine, in which case we have to act fast and send him to theatre for surgery before he loses the blood supply to the affected part. His heart rate and breathing are rapid, so I think it's a fair assumption that this is not a minor problem.'

'You're probably right.' She sent him a fleeting glance, assessing the taut lines of his face and the straight-backed, determined way he was moving towards the central desk to go and set things in motion.

'When you've sorted all that out, you should perhaps go and take a break. You've been on the go all morning, and it would do you good to spend some time in the staff lounge, maybe getting to know people better, and finding out about everything that's going on.'

'I already know what's going on,' he said. 'I take time to update myself every morning and read all the memos that my secretary puts my way. I know when all the meetings are taking place and who's pencilled in on the rota. I don't need to take time out when there are more pressing claims on my attention.'

'Oh, that's no fun at all.' She looked at him askance. 'James brought in some pasties in celebration of his patient with the subdural haematoma making a good recovery—well, that was his excuse, anyway. I happen to know he likes the girl who works in the bakery...he always says it's the smell of the food that draws him in there, but he spends way longer than necessary chatting to her.'

Sam laughed. 'You know all about the secret lives of the doctors and nurses around here, don't you? They all seem to confide in you.'

'Ah, well, no one keeps a secret for long in here. This place is a hotbed of gossip, you know. And that's another reason why you should go along to the staff lounge. They're all longing to know everything there is to know about you and how you came to be at Ashvale. Rumour has it that you bribed all the members of the board to win your place here, and you promised them you'd deliver enough savings to keep the Heritage running for a year.'

His mouth dropped open. 'You can't be serious?'

'Nah. Just kidding.' She grinned. 'But I think you should take my advice and go and mix with your colleagues a bit more. The pace here is hectic at times, and you'd do well to wind down whenever the opportunity arises. Besides, you'll get along far better with your workforce if you try to relate to them outside of their everyday duties.' She sent him a quick glance, trying unsuccessfully to gauge his reaction, before picking out a chart from the pile on the desk. She briefly skimmed the contents.

Sam, though, instead of taking her comments in the light-hearted fashion they were meant, was shaking his head in disbelief. She frowned. That didn't bode too well, did it?

He reached for the phone. 'Radiology,' he said into the mouthpiece. 'I need to send an infant to you for a scan.' He turned to Ruby while the clerk at the other end of the line tried to contact the radiologist.

'In case you've forgotten,' he told her in a dry tone, 'I'm

the head of department here. I didn't get to this position without knowing how to conduct myself, and I'm sorry if I haven't quite managed to come up to your expectations. You just have to remember that the whole unit is straining under a heavier than usual burden right now, and I have to prioritise my time to the best effect. Unfortunately, that doesn't leave me a lot of time to socialize.' He turned back to his phone call as the clerk came back on the line.

Ruby drew in a deep breath at the snub. She was taken aback by his attitude, but she couldn't really blame him for his riposte, could she, even though she'd only been trying to help. Maybe she *had* gone too far.

In fact, she couldn't really see why she was bothering at all attempting to help him settle into the department when she had problems of her own to contend with.

She walked away from the desk and left him to his phone conversation. Maybe she would give her neighbour, Claire, a ring and find out if her sister had turned up at the house. It would cheer her up no end to know that Becky's mother was safe and well and planning on taking care of her little daughter.

No such relief was in the offing, though. Claire said there hadn't been any news of Sophie, and Ruby then checked in with the police, who informed her there had been no more sightings. They wanted to know if there were any local places where Sophie would go to lie low, but Ruby simply couldn't think of any. She had already tried looking in all the old familiar haunts from their childhood to no avail.

She went to check on Becky at lunchtime with a heavy heart. The nursery matron said that she had been fine, but the child was tearful when Ruby arrived, wanting to be picked up and comforted, and Ruby sensed that she didn't want her to leave.

'Mm…mm…mm…' Becky mouthed against Ruby's shoulder. She put her small fist into her mouth and pressed down on it, becoming agitated.

'I think she must be teething,' the woman said. 'Perhaps her gums are a bit sore.'

'Maybe.' Ruby felt as miserable as the child. She didn't want to leave her here with strangers, but in a short time she had to go back down to A&E, so what choice did she have? Meanwhile, Becky was clinging to her, unwilling to let go.

'I'll sit down with you and show you a picture book, shall I, poppet?' she said after a while. 'Let's see if that will soothe you.'

She sat in a cosy armchair and nestled the infant in her arms, showing her the bright illustrations in a soft, waterproof bath book. 'There's a duck,' she said, pointing to the mallard swimming on a reed-edged pond. 'Just like the one at Gran's country place.'

'Nan-nan,' Becky said. 'Nan-nan.'

'That's right. You remember, don't you?' She turned the page. 'And there's a bird sitting on the fence.'

Becky became excited looking at the pictures, her eyes widening with concentration, her arms and legs moving in eager expectation, her hands closing into small fists as though she would touch it and grasp it with her fingers.

'You like that, don't you?' Ruby said. 'I think you probably want to hold it yourself.'

She let Becky clutch the book, and after a while the infant drew it closer, testing its softness with her mouth. Ruby laughed softly. 'I might have known you would try to eat it,' she said.

Some time later, she settled the baby down in a crib, leaving her to explore the pages by herself.

'You slip away while she's preoccupied,' the matron said. 'I expect she'll be ready for a nap before too long.'

Ruby nodded and went out to take the lift down to A&E. She was sad to leave Becky and a little overwhelmed by the tasks that lay ahead of her over the next few days: moving to the smallholding and waiting for Sophie to return.

Concentrating on her work would at least help to numb the edges of her unhappiness. She went in search of the lab results for the man who had felt his legs buckle under him and found that Nick Dryden's blood test showed that his red blood cell count was low.

She went to check up on him. 'Hello again, Nick,' she said. 'How are you feeling?'

He held out a hand palm down and moved it from side to side. 'So-so,' he said.

'Hmmm. I'd like to check your blood pressure again if that's okay with you,' she murmured.

He nodded.

The pressure was falling, she discovered, and his pulse was faster than the last reading.

She asked him about his daily routine. 'You're not working at the moment, are you?'

He shook his head. 'I was laid off after the car accident.'

'And has anything happened to you in the last week or so?'

'Nothing, really. The most exciting thing that happened to me I went to a mate's house with some friends the day before yesterday, and we watched the football match on TV. Our team won, so we were well made up.'

'Sounds good.' Ruby gave a brief smile.

'Yeah. I stood up to cheer and lock arms with my mate and fell over the table. Caught myself right here.' He ran a hand over the upper part of his abdomen and grinned. 'Too much lager. Made me grunt a bit at the time, but it's more or less okay now. It's a bit sore.'

Ruby was beginning to be slightly concerned. 'I think we'll do an abdominal CT scan to see if anything untoward is going on,' she told him. 'I'll arrange for the nurse to take you down to radiology as soon as she's free.'

She left the room and made the arrangements with Michelle, leaving Nick in the care of the nurse while she wrote up his radiology form. A few minutes later, as she was checking details of her other patients, Sam came to find her.

'I've just seen Michelle preparing to take your patient down to radiology,' he said. 'She tells me that you've ordered an abdominal CT scan.'

'That's right. Why, is there a problem?'

He frowned. 'You do know that he's a regular here, don't you? I've taken a look at his notes, and it's clear that Dr Stanford believed he was simply a drug seeker. He may well have suffered an accident at some time, but there's no evidence of permanent injury on all the scans and X-rays that have been done.'

'Maybe so, but I prefer to do the tests anyway. Something about him doesn't seem quite right. It doesn't add up.'

He made a short laugh. 'Yes, well, I can understand that. You do realise that he was the one who almost knocked you over the other day outside the hospital…don't you remember? He didn't even stop to apologise.'

Recognition dawned all at once, and her mouth dropped open a fraction. 'Ah, I knew there was something about him that bothered me. Yes, I remember now.'

'Good. Then perhaps you'll think twice about wasting resources on someone who's probably just here to get his hands on stronger painkillers. He's done it before, several times. It's more than likely he's taking you for a ride, Ruby. He probably thinks you're a soft touch.'

'Well, it's possible, I suppose.' She looked him in the eye, her grey gaze smoky with annoyance. 'Still, I decided to take his claims at face value and examined him accordingly, and my feeling is that there may be something wrong with him.' She drew herself up to her full height. 'Last time I looked, my qualifications said I was a specialist registrar—so I think that gives me enough leeway to act on my gut instinct, don't you?' It was a low trick, but he had pulled rank with her earlier, and she didn't see why she should allow him to browbeat her on this.

He didn't react in quite the way she'd expected. There was no rising hauteur or demand for her to retract. Instead, he held up his hands in a gesture of conciliation. 'Okay. Whoa there. Steady.' He let his arms fall to his sides. 'I suppose I deserved that response, but the truth is, I'm not trying to tell you what to do. I'm just saying you should bear in mind that he's probably just after a prescription for stronger narcotics. He's had a few X-rays and CT scans, and nothing has ever showed up.'

'I'll take that on board,' she said. 'Thank you for pointing it out. And now I need to go and see to my other patients…unless there was something else you wanted?'

He made an exaggerated movement away from her, backing off and indicating with a swish of his hands that she was free to go on her way. 'Don't let me stop you,' he said.

'I won't.'

She was in no mood to parry words with Sam Boyd any longer. In fact, one way or another, she was coming close to the end of her tether. Over the course of the last couple of weeks she'd lost the job she'd set her heart on, the department looked as if it was heading down the road to closure, her sister had disappeared, leaving her with a baby to look after, and as soon as she left here, she had to go and take over the reins of her grandparents' smallholding. And that was without battling to stay composed while doing the work of several people because of staff shortages.

It dawned on her as she went about her work that there was only one course of action to take…and there was no time like the present to see it through. As soon as she had a free moment, she stopped by the human resources office and informed the admin clerk that she would not be renewing her contract.

'I'll pass the information on to your head of department,' the clerk said, 'but I expect you'll want to do that personally, too.' She carefully checked the details on the computer. 'You still have a couple of weeks' leave due,' the woman said. 'You'll need to take it right away.'

'Okay. I'll do that.'

Ruby left the office a few minutes later. A feeling of relief washed over her now that it was done, and all she had to do now was go in search of Sam and let him know what was happening. When she couldn't find him, she told his secretary what she was doing and left a note on the desk in his office before going back to work.

The calm feeling stayed with her, even when Michelle came hurrying over to her.

'Ruby, you need to come right away. It's your patient, Mr Dryden—his scan shows a nasty laceration to his spleen. He's bleeding internally, and the radiologist says he needs to go to theatre right away.'

'Okay,' she said. 'I'll organise it. Thanks, Michelle.'

Somehow, it wasn't unexpected. She studied the radiology films and then gathered a team together, making sure that her patient was prepped for surgery. She would have preferred to do a repair operation, but, as things turned out, the damage to his spleen was too great, and she had no choice but to remove it.

It meant that his health would need to be monitored on a regular basis from now on since he could be more prone to suffer infections, but at least disaster had been averted, and his life had been saved.

When she came back down from theatre some time later, she wrote up the patient's notes and arranged for him to be admitted to a surgical ward.

'You'll probably need to stay in hospital for a few days,' she told him when the nurse came to transfer him over there. 'After that, you should be fine, but you'll need to see your GP to arrange follow-up appointments.'

'Thanks,' he said. He was still pale and drowsy from the operation. 'The nurse told me you saved my life.'

She smiled. 'You're welcome. That's what I'm here for, to do whatever I can.'

Michelle wheeled him away with the help of a porter, and Ruby headed back towards the central desk.

'You see,' she told Sam when she discovered him there, rummaging through the patients' files. 'I knew things were not quite right with our Mr Dryden.' The urge to say I told you so had the better of her. 'You should take note of what my instincts tell me. I don't make these decisions lightly.'

'You're right,' he said, giving her a wry smile. 'It's because of your actions that he's here to tell the tale.' His gaze drifted over her. 'And I'll bet you're going to make me pay big time for my remarks, aren't you? I expect you'll be gloating all through next week.'

She shook her head. 'Not at all,' she murmured. 'In fact, I won't be here…I start my annual leave as of tomorrow. And I've been over to personnel and told them I won't be renewing my contract.'

He sent her a stunned look. 'I don't believe it,' he ground out on a terse note. 'How come I didn't know anything about this?'

'It was a last-minute decision on my part, I admit,' she said, 'but I did let it be known some time ago that I wasn't sure about staying on here as registrar once my contract came to an end.' She gave him a sweet smile. 'Perhaps you should have read the memo,' she said.

CHAPTER FOUR

RUBY gazed at the phone, willing it to ring. All she needed was a message from Sophie to say that she was well and that she would be coming back home just as soon as she could get her head together. Just one call to give her peace of mind…was that too much to ask? At least the police would be able to track Sophie's movements from a phone call, wouldn't they?

Frustration tugged her stomach into tight knots. It had been over a week now, and there had been no sign of her sister, no clue as to where she might be. The agony of not knowing what had happened to her was unbearable. Was she safe? Was she well? There was no rhyme or reason behind her disappearance. Sophie loved her baby, so why would she go? Nothing made sense any more.

'Da-da,' Becky chanted, looking up at Ruby from the comfort of the mat on the floor, where she was enjoying her newfound ability to sit up straight all by herself. She was holding out a circular teething ring, and now she quickly lifted her arms up and down in unison as though she would bang the floor with the ring and hear the rattling noise it made.

Ruby's mouth turned down at the corners. 'No, baby,' she murmured, kneeling down beside her. 'No Da-da.' She gave a soft sigh. 'No anybody, except me. I guess that means we're stuck with one another, but I'm okay with it if you are.'

Becky gurgled, biting down on the toy and coming out with an excited babble of baby talk, so that Ruby smiled. 'You're absolutely right,' she told the infant. 'We'll just have to make the best of things, won't we? At least we get to stay in this lovely farmhouse and enjoy the comfort of a log fire of an evening.'

The one consolation in all of this was that she had the opportunity to spend time with Becky, playing with her and cuddling her to her heart's content. If Becky wondered where her mother had gone, Ruby guessed it was in those fleeting moments when a door creaked and she looked up expectantly, waiting to see if Sophie would walk in, or on those occasions when Ruby laid her in her cot so that she could take a nap. Then the child would give a small frown and look around as though sensing that something was missing and all was not as it should be.

She could not explain to her what was going on. All she could do was offer comfort and kisses in between the time she spent tending to the animals and weeding around the vegetables that grew in abundance on this rambling four-acre plot.

'And I do look forward to sitting by that huge old fireplace this evening,' she told Becky. 'Truth is, I'm too exhausted to do anything else.'

She looked around the cosy living room, pleasingly furnished with sofas and chairs in softly textured upholstery, and lifted here and there with splashes of bright colour in the cushions. The drapes were beautifully elegant, providing a sumptuous backdrop to the fine pieces of solid golden oak furniture. Wide French doors looked out on to the landscaped gardens beyond. 'It could be so restful here if it wasn't for worrying about you and your mother and about the animals getting sick.'

And, if she was honest with herself, wasn't there also the faint tinge of regret for the career that she had left behind? How were they coping without her at the hospital? Had Sam recovered from his dismay at seeing her go? Even as she had teased him about not being on top of the staffing rota, she had been aware of a twinge of guilt. She had left the decision too much to the last minute, and now he was left to cope with the beleaguered department on his own. Would he be able to lift it out of the doldrums without help?

Maybe she had been too hasty in giving it all up? A week or more of reflection had left her feeling regretful about the colleagues she had left behind and uncertain about which path to take to secure her future happiness.

The doorbell rang, and Becky looked puzzled, her lips moving on a questioning sound as though she was asking who it could be.

'It's probably Craig, the vet, come to look at the pony,' Ruby told her. 'I asked him if he could spare the time to check him out…the ducks too, because, as you know, nothing is working out as it should just lately.'

Becky frowned, and Ruby lightly ruffled her dark gold curls. 'Don't worry about it, poppet. Your aunty is not quite herself, but she'll get better.'

She stood up and went to answer the door, startled to discover that it wasn't the vet who stood in the porch, but Sam Boyd, immaculately dressed as ever, though in slightly more casual attire, wearing perfectly fitting dark trousers, a crisp linen shirt in a pleasing shade of blue, and a soft suede jacket that he had left unzipped.

'Oh,' she said, her eyes widening. 'This is a surprise. I thought you were the vet come to look at the animals.'

He appeared to be confused for a moment, then lightly ran the palm of his hand over his chest. 'No, it's me, Sam, as far as I know. I never did take any veterinary exams. I always thought animals were way too unpredictable to make good patients. Cute, maybe, and loveable to a certain extent, but definitely not my calling.'

'You're incorrigible,' she said, moving back from the door and ushering him inside the house. 'Come in. Watch your step; there are hazards everywhere…toys, baby walker, linen baskets—I haven't quite got the hang of this baby business yet.'

'You haven't?'

'No.'

He looked puzzled, and then that expression changed to a frown as he stepped around the baby-changing unit that partly blocked the hallway.

'It's too heavy for me to move by myself,' she offered in explanation. 'It's solid wood, and the cupboard part of it is full of baby equipment. I suppose I really need to get around to emptying it at some point and put it where it would best fit. Someone dropped it off for me, and I couldn't quite decide where it needed to go.'

'Oh, I see. Well, I can always move it for you if you tell me where.'

It was fairly obvious that he didn't see at all, but Ruby ignored all that and ushered him into the large farmhouse kitchen. 'Thanks. Maybe we could shift it together later. I've decided it can go in the utility room just off the kitchen.' She waved a hand in the direction of the L-shaped annexe. 'There's a space just big enough for it by the wall.'

She went over to the worktop at the side of the kitchen. 'I was just about to make a pot of tea and grab a sandwich,' she told him, picking up the kettle and taking it over to the sink. 'Would you like something to eat and drink?' He looked as though he could do with taking time out for a while, and whatever pressing problem had brought him here could probably wait while she brewed up.

He was busy looking around the room as she spoke, absorbing its wide proportions, his glance drifting over the sturdy oak table and chairs and the homely touches in the colourful curtains and small items of linen that were lying around. He seemed a trifle tense, out of place in this homely farmhouse, as though he was uncomfortable about something or other. Perhaps he hadn't wanted to come here to see her, but found it necessary for some reason…problems at work, maybe?

'Uh, thanks,' he said. He seemed a touch taken aback by her offer. Perhaps he wasn't used to impromptu invitations of that sort, but Ruby had been hard at work all day, and she was both hungry and thirsty and didn't see the point in waiting to satisfy those needs.

'I have some home-made pizza slices that are still warm from the oven,' she told him as she filled the kettle with water, 'and there are some scones that I baked this morning.' It was fairly late in the afternoon, and she guessed he might have been caught up for most of the day in the fast-paced, energy-draining routine of the A&E department.

He brightened a little. 'That would be great if it's not too much trouble. I didn't get the chance to eat at the hospital.'

She nodded. 'I heard on the news that there was an industrial accident in one of the town factories. I thought they would probably send most of the injured to Ashvale.'

'Yes, they did.'

She switched on the kettle and then glanced at him briefly. 'I noticed that you would rarely take time out to go and eat a proper meal if we were busy at work. If it hadn't been for my policy of having a trolley laden with snacks on hand, I don't know how you would have fared. You always have that lean and hungry look.' She turned towards the living room. 'Anyway, sit yourself down at the table. I'll just go and fetch Becky. She can sit in her high chair and nibble on a rusk while we eat.'

He did as she suggested, pulling out a chair and carefully removing the large, floppy-eared, patchwork quilt rabbit from the seat, giving it an uncertain look before placing it down on an unused part of the worktop. She sent him a benign smile.

There weren't too many empty areas left since she had been far too busy to clear away all the fruits of her labour today.

There was a wicker basket of eggs that should have been stowed away in the fridge, a few jars of home-made preserve that her mother had dropped off that morning, and a selection of toys that she had kept handy to amuse Becky while she'd attempted to deal with various tasks during the day.

'How do you cope with all th—?' He broke off mid-sentence as though he'd suddenly thought better of what he was about to say.

'With all this clutter?' she supplied helpfully. 'It's easy. I simply ignore it. I have to, otherwise I'd probably go quietly mad.'

She hurried away to go and fetch Becky, leaving him sitting there with a bemused look on his face.

Becky seemed pleased to see him when Ruby carried her into the room a few moments later. She broke into a babble of excited chatter and tried to grab a handful of his hair as she passed by.

He tilted his head to one side, taking evasive action, but unfortunately he wasn't quite fast enough.

'No, no…' Ruby admonished the baby, gently unfastening her small fist from the silky strands of his thick, dark hair. His hair was clean and springy in texture, and Ruby was taken unawares by the series of tiny electric shocks that ran along her wrist and arm as her fingers brushed lightly against the strands. Her nervous system was too highly strung for such intimate contact, obviously. In fact, the whole notion that her refined, meticulous former boss was sitting in her grandparents' country kitchen seemed more than a touch bizarre.

'Leave Sam be, Becky,' she murmured, getting herself together. 'He's not used to our exuberant country ways.' She placed the infant in her high chair and Becky proceeded to noisily bang her rattle on the food tray, laughing with glee at the din she was making.

Sam winced at the noise and after a moment or two thoughtfully handed her the oversized rabbit, so that peace reigned for a while as she hugged it close. He looked pleasantly surprised that his strategy had worked, and Ruby gave a soft laugh.

'Now you see what I have to put up with all day,' she murmured. Glancing at him, she added, 'You seem to have been working on your technique with youngsters. Distraction tactics tend to work, don't they?' She poured tea and pushed a generously sized cup towards him, adding a plate of pizza slices and a bowl of salad to the table, along with a plate and cutlery. 'Help yourself. We don't go in for table manners and etiquette around here. Old habits die hard. It's a case of grab it and eat while you have the chance...much the same as at the hospital.'

He did as she suggested, helping himself to a pizza slice, and she added conversationally, 'How are things at the hospital? Is there any news of the infant who came in with abdominal pain? How's he doing? Last I heard, you were planning on sending him for surgery.'

'That's right. It turned out that he had an obstruction in his intestine, as we thought, so I called for the specialist surgeon to come and take a look at him. He operated later that same day, and now the little boy's recovering on the paediatric ward.'

'And he's doing well?'

'Yes, he is.'

'Good, I'm glad of that. It's a relief to know that at least some things manage to turn out all right.' She handed Becky a rusk, removing the rabbit gently from her grasp, and then buttered herself a fruit scone, putting it to her lips and taking a bite. She didn't sit down—Becky was likely to need attention, and it was easier if she was by her side.

'Do I detect a note of strain in your tone?' he asked, sending her a thoughtful glance. He took a bite of pizza, savouring the cheese and tomato as though it was a whole new experience. Then he licked the sauce from his lips with the tip of his tongue, and she had the feeling that he was trying to work out what made the flavours so special. It was probably the delicate blend of herbs she had added. Ruby watched him in fascination, lost in a world of her own until he asked quietly, 'Have things here not turned out quite as you hoped?'

She came back to earth with a jolt. 'I'm not exactly sure what I was expecting,' she answered, wiping her hands on a paper towel. 'All I know is that one of the ponies is off his food, one or two of the ducks have a problem with their wing feathers, and the hens are not laying as well as they might. I suspect some of them are a bit old now and have given up on trying.'

'Oh, I see.' His brows drew together. 'I suppose you'll take them off to market and bring in some new ones, will you?'

'Certainly not.' Her voice rose on a note of indignation, and she glared at him, affronted that he should suggest such a thing. 'I wouldn't dream of sending them away. They'll stay here and live out their lives on the farm.'

He laughed. 'This is not meant to be a commercial enterprise, then? Just a happy-go-lucky country-living type enterprise?'

'We're just playing at being farmers, you mean?' She let her shoulders drop and gave an amused smile. At least he'd begun to relax a little. Perhaps the food and hot tea was all that he needed to help him to unwind. 'You make it sound as though we're a bunch of country yokels. I have to tell you, I'm not quite ready for the battered hat and straw between the teeth just yet.'

She spread home-made raspberry preserve onto another scone. 'In fact, my grandparents do make a small living from the fruit crops they grow, and then there's the honey they get from the beehives. Sometimes, through the summer months, they open the farm up to visitors—family groups, mostly. There are lots of activities youngsters can get into—like pond dipping, or swinging on the rope in the hay barn. There's a small playground area too. And of course, there are the animals to see. They even have pony rides sometimes.'

She bit into the scone, leaning back against the nearby worktop, lost for a moment in sheer enjoyment of the sweet fruit. 'I could show you around the place if you like—or at least some of it.'

'Thanks. That would be good.' Sam's gaze drifted over her, his expression strangely unreadable as she arched her back briefly to relieve muscles that were stiff after a day's work on the small farm. She gave a small frown, wondering if he was contemplating the slightly generous nature of her curves, given her obvious enjoyment of pastries and the like. She wasn't particularly slender, but, then again, she wasn't overweight either, and her jeans fitted her snugly, as did the cotton top that left her midriff bare whenever she stretched.

She straightened up. Perhaps it was her naked midsection that had caused his glance to wander.

He averted his gaze. 'So once you've managed to sort out the animals' problems, things will be fairly straightforward, I imagine,' he said in the small silence that had arisen. 'You'll be able to settle to this way of life.'

'I don't know about that.' Her mouth made a downward curve. 'Becky's teething, which means she's constantly dribbling and intermittently crying because her gums are sore. And on top of that I've discovered a leak in the roof that's causing a damp patch on one of the bedroom walls, and the central heating's on the blink. Not that I need it very much right now, but the nights are becoming cooler, and it would be nice to be able to take the chill off the place.'

He was listening intently, but now he paused, his teacup halfway to his lips, so that her gaze was drawn to the long, bronzed fingers that circled the handle. The back of his hand was covered with a light smattering of golden hair, and, as he moved to set the cup down again, she caught a glimpse of the distinctive watch that circled his strong wrist beneath the beautifully laundered cuff of his shirt.

For just a second or two she was captivated by the sheer maleness that he exuded. He didn't have to say a word. He simply sat there in her kitchen, looking overwhelmingly masculine, and she found herself thinking that of all the men in the world he was an example of one who could make women go weak at the knees without even trying.

She couldn't imagine why her thoughts were wandering in that direction. She wasn't in any way about to succumb to his subtle blend of magnetism, was she? He was the total opposite of everything she stood for.

Besides, she wasn't looking for a man in her life, not after Tom had let her down by showing himself in his true colours. That had been an eye-opener. It had taught her that you never quite knew where you were with men. They seemed to be everything you could want, and then, just when you let yourself relax and accept that this might possibly be the real thing, they turned your world upside down and headed off for greener pastures.

She frowned. Hadn't the same thing happened with Sophie? Except that Becky's father had turned out to be a married man looking for a temporary diversion, and poor Sophie had no idea until it was too late. No, she decided, men were not to be trusted with something as tender and special as a woman's affection. They didn't appear to appreciate it.

She pulled herself together and distracted herself by gathering up a broken piece of rusk from the high chair's food tray and handing it to Becky. 'Here you are,' she told her. 'See if you can finish it all.'

'I can see that you have your hands full with the baby, as well as the house and the farm,' Sam said, 'so anything else is an added burden. Isn't your husband able to sort these things out for you?' He gave her a searching look. 'It seems to me you have more than enough to contend with around here…and that's without taking into account what you've already given up—the rewarding career you've left behind.'

She returned his gaze. 'I don't have a husband,' she said.

He frowned, shooting a glance at her bare ring finger. 'I'm sorry. I didn't realise…' He was clearly thrown by that revelation, but he recovered himself, appearing to mull things over. 'That must make life doubly difficult for you, having to take care of your baby on your own. It's perhaps no wonder that you found it all too much of an effort to go on with your job.'

'Actually…' she sat down at last and faced him squarely '…it isn't like that at all. I mean, yes, I had to take time out to look after the baby…but Becky isn't mine. She's my sister's baby—only Sophie went off a week or so ago, without warning, and there's no one else who can take care of her child.'

His expression was stunned. 'Is she coming back?'

Ruby shrugged. 'I don't know. The police are looking for her, but so far they haven't managed to find her.'

He was silent for a moment or two. 'That's shocking news…you must be very worried.'

She nodded. 'I am, though I'm holding on to the belief that nothing bad has happened to her. She seemed to be quite confused just before she left, and I think she may have needed some time on her own to sort herself out.'

'That still leaves you having to pick up the pieces.' He was frowning now. 'Surely you could have let the authorities look after the infant? I imagine they wouldn't have much trouble finding her a foster family. Why would you have to ruin your life by taking on her care?'

Ruby's gaze narrowed on him. 'You obviously have no understanding of how relationships work,' she said, keeping her voice low and even but unable to hide the thread of exasperation.

He raised a dark brow. 'I know enough to understand that

your sister went off and left her child. What kind of mother would do that? And why should you take over the reins? Becky's gorgeous, I grant you, but when it comes down to it, she isn't your problem.'

'Maybe I don't see it that way.' He really ought to have read the warning signs that were sparking in her eyes because his cavalier attitude was beginning to rile her. She was usually incredibly even-tempered, but the thought that anyone could dismiss Becky as someone to be parcelled off into local authority care made her thoroughly irritable. 'Families are important,' she said, emphasising the words. 'Don't you see that? Wouldn't you do the same for your family?'

He frowned. 'Perhaps those loyalties aren't so important to me, but, then, my family isn't a close-knit one. Don't get me wrong—we have a great bond and affection for one another, but we don't live in each other's pockets. My parents are away looking after their business interests abroad for a good part of the year, and my younger brother is working up in Scotland. We keep in touch, obviously, but generally we're pretty much self-reliant. I'm able and willing to look after the family's country estate while they're away, but I doubt that any one of them would call on me to do more than I do already.'

She sent him a guarded look. His outlook on life was so different to hers. She was part of a loving, caring, hands-on family, whereas he seemed to prefer his independence. Was that the reason he was uncomfortable with the general camaraderie back at the hospital? No wonder he acted the way he did. Surely, his comments were the key to his whole personality? He was totally self-sufficient, needing no one—instead, he was a law unto himself, concentrating only on the job in hand as though it was all that mattered.

She frowned. And what was that about a country estate? That conjured up all kinds of images in her mind, but she batted them away and concentrated instead on the issue at hand. 'Well, I don't feel the same way at all. My family mean everything to me, and we always help one another out in any way we can. My sister is ill, and I'm worried about her, and I feel a responsibility towards her baby. Sophie can't possibly be thinking straight or she wouldn't have left.'

She stood up, knowing that if she stayed still her emotions would most likely well up inside her and bubble over, with disastrous consequences. She didn't want to say something she might regret later. Instead, she handed Becky another piece of rusk that had broken off from the main biscuit. The little girl's mouth was smeared with gooey cereal, and her fingers and palms were covered in moist rusk from where she had dabbled her hands in her food.

'That still doesn't make her child your concern.'

'But I want her to be my concern.' She glowered at him from beneath her lashes, and this time he must finally have taken note of the sharp edge to her voice and the glitter of her gaze because his eyes widened a fraction.

'She's family,' Ruby went on, 'which gives me a strong reason for wanting to take care of her. Added to that, I'm of an age where I'm wondering if having a career is maybe not the be all and end all of life, after all. Perhaps I'm missing out on the biggest part of what being a woman is all about. I hope it's not the case, but it occurs to me that I might never experience the joy of looking after a child of my own, so taking care of my sister's baby has to come somewhere close to the ideal.'

He looked at her in astonishment, as if he thought she had taken leave of her senses. 'So your career—everything you've worked for all these years—is just to be thrown by the wayside on a whim. Do you really plan on giving it all up?'

She frowned. 'I think you already know the answer to that, don't you?'

He shook his head. 'I'm finding it hard to accept that you

can turn your back on it so easily. You're extremely good at your job. You're a paediatrician who specialises in A&E, and that's a rare and valuable combination. We need you at the hospital, Ruby. There's no one who can take your place. You have a wonderful talent for getting the best out of people. That's why I came here today, to ask if you would consider coming back to work.'

'I thought that might be the reason why you were here.' She stood up and went to run a flannel under the water at the sink so that she could wipe Becky's face and hands. It gave her something to do, to lessen the impact his words were having on her equilibrium. He was pointing out things that she had already turned over in her mind, areas of frustration that she had battled to overcome.

He got to his feet and started towards her, but Becky was not about to let this interesting person out of her range without a fight. The baby leaned towards him, grasping his jacket in her small fist, and then she buried her face in the suede, drawing it to her mouth.

'Oh dear. I'm so sorry,' Ruby said, looking at him in consternation. 'I should have warned you. She does that all the while. Everything goes straight to her mouth.'

He drew back, carefully disengaging himself from Becky's attentions, and, deprived of her newfound sensory toy, the little girl began to wail. Her face crumpled, her cheeks reddened, and tears began to trickle down her face.

Sam's expression was so stricken that it was almost comical. 'What am I supposed to do?' he said, looking to Ruby for an answer that would put a quick end to the ear-shattering noise.

Ruby's shoulders moved in an awkward fashion. 'Don't ask me,' she said. 'I'm a beginner at this, the same as you.' She shifted the flannel about in her hands in an agony of indecision. What should she wipe first—Sam's jacket or Becky's face?

He took the matter out of her hands by going over to the worktop and grabbing a handful of kitchen towels. While he removed the mess from his jacket, Ruby attended to Becky, trying to soothe the child and wipe her clean at the same time.

'It's not so bad, Becky,' she murmured softly. 'I expect you wouldn't really have liked the taste of his jacket. Anyway, I think you're probably tired, aren't you? I'll clean you up and pop you in your crib for a while, and then you can hold on to Bunny Rabbit and tell him all your troubles.'

She glanced at Sam while she attended to the baby's face and hands. He had managed to clean the worst of the mess from his jacket, but the soft suede was wet now, and she guessed it would stiffen as it dried.

'Don't worry about it,' he said, reading her thoughts. 'Just concentrate on seeing to Becky, and then maybe we can talk.'

She nodded. She guessed he couldn't think straight while the loud wailing was going on in the background, and she felt pretty much the same way. That was why the crying device worked so well where babies were concerned. You had to deal with it as a priority if you were to stay sane.

'I'll put her to bed,' she said, lifting the child out of the seat. 'You could go and take a look around outside if you like, and I'll catch up with you in a while. If I hook the baby monitor to the belt loop on my jeans, we can take a short walk in the grounds, and I'll still know if she needs my attention.'

'Okay. Take your time.' Perhaps he sensed that she was suddenly stressed because he smiled and held out the patchwork rabbit to Becky, almost like a peace offering.

Becky's eyes widened, and she stopped crying, hiccupping instead, and looking at him with a guarded expression that said her opinion of him was under review.

Ruby whisked the child away, taking her to the bedroom upstairs and settling her down in her cot. She set the video monitor to play soft lullabies to soothe her to sleep, and after a few minutes, when Becky's eyelids were beginning to droop, she crept quietly out of the room.

When she went back into the kitchen, she discovered that Sam had cleared away the food and crockery from the table, and all was relatively spick and span. He had also moved the changing unit into the utility room.

His thoughtfulness started a warm glow inside her, and she hurried outside to go in search of him.

She found him out by the paddock where the two Shetland ponies, Candy and Toffee, had been put out to pasture. Toffee, a seven-year-old with a lovely chestnut coat and silver mane and tail, sauntered towards the fence as Ruby went to stand beside Sam, but the smaller five-year-old stayed where he was, head down, looking miserable and out of sorts. He was a soft brown colour, with a white nose patch.

'Thanks for clearing up for me,' she said, 'and for moving the changing table.'

'You're welcome.' Sam turned his attention back to the ponies. 'I guess the smaller one is the pony the vet's coming to see?' he enquired. 'He doesn't look too happy, does he?'

Ruby shook her head. 'It's a tummy upset, I think.' She sighed. 'I told Craig over the phone what the problem was. I haven't done anything different in handling him, or added anything to his feed, so I don't have any idea what might be causing his symptoms.'

She frowned. 'I would hate for things to go wrong here just because I'm in charge, but I'm a novice at all this. I love being here, but it takes some getting used to, making sure that I follow all the feeding and grooming routines. Gran wrote me out a schedule, but there's a lot of ground to cover, and only so many hours in the day. I suppose it could be that my timing is off, and that's why Candy is ill. It's probably the reason the ducks are losing their feathers too.'

Perhaps it was her sorrowful tone that diverted his attention from the pony. His gaze shifted over her, warmth shimmering in the depths of his blue-grey eyes. 'You shouldn't blame yourself. I'm sure you're doing the very best you can.' He reached for her, lightly stroking her arms in a gesture of sympathy. 'It can't be easy for you with young Becky taking up so much of your time.'

'Yes, well, none of us had counted on that.' She was very conscious of those hands circling her arms. She felt the warmth of his fingers on her bare skin, and her whole body was beginning to stir in response to that gentle touch.

'Isn't there anyone else who could help out—your parents, perhaps?'

She nodded. 'They've been doing as much as they can. They're both working, but they come over every day to take over for a while and give me a bit of a break. It's the only way I can find the time to write my magazine articles or fit in the Internet work.'

He shook his head in wonder. 'You're a truly amazing woman, Ruby.' His mouth curved, lightening his features in a way that made her heart begin to thump in an erratic rhythm. 'I knew you were special when I saw how well you handled things at the meeting on that first day we met. You stuck to your guns and had no intention of backing down, even with a roomful of people looking on. I knew then that you were up for a challenge, and when I saw you at work in A&E, it only confirmed it for me. You have a way of meeting situations head on, without letting the pressure get to you.' He frowned. 'That's why I couldn't understand you giving up on us at the hospital.'

'I didn't give up on you. I just couldn't see how I could do right by my family and give the whole of my attention to my work as well. Something had to give, and it turned out that it was my responsibility to A&E that had to fall by the wayside. I'm only one person, and I don't believe I'm indispensable.'

His mouth flattened. 'I don't agree with that. You have a unique way of motivating everyone at work. They all miss you.'

She gave a soft sigh. 'I'm sorry about that. But the fact of the matter is, you'd already decided that you could lay off staff and still make a go of it, whereas I wasn't so sure I could work under those conditions.' He was stirring up emotions in her that she would rather lie dormant: restlessness, guilt and a faint sorrow for what she had abandoned. She was torn by all the demands being made on her. There was frustration, too, a sense of helplessness, of not knowing how to do things differently, that made her want to turn away from him and avoid his censure.

He wouldn't let her turn away, though. Instead, he drew her closer to him, so that she had no choice but to listen to what he had to say. She was all too aware of the warmth emanating from him, of the sheer male energy and drive that gave him an inherent authority over everyone who happened to come within his orbit. 'That's just it, Ruby,' he murmured. 'I'm discovering every day exactly how much the department needs you at its helm. I can only do so much, but with you on my team we can work wonders.'

'It isn't possible,' she said. 'I've made my choice.'

'And if your sister was to come back within a day or so, how will things be then? You'll have given up everything…and for what? A few weeks of being able to cuddle your niece and commune with nature? I don't believe that's a strong enough reason to give it all up, Ruby.'

'It's more than that. It's peace of mind, taking the chance to opt out from the mindless whirl of administrative solutions that make no sense.' She was finding it hard to think straight while he was holding her this way. His hands were slowly smoothing over the silk of her skin, as though he would mesmerise her and coax her into accepting what he had to say.

'You're confused, emotionally torn, and I think that means

you aren't thinking rationally. I don't believe you really want to give up everything you've worked so hard to gain.' He studied her closely, his gaze meshing with hers. 'If I were to offer you a solution to all your troubles, would you consider coming back to the hospital?'

She blinked in shock. 'What solution could there possibly be?' She was startled enough by his suggestion that she moved away from the paddock fence and began to walk slowly along the footpath towards the duck pond. He went with her, not letting go of her, but sliding his arm around her shoulders in a warm embrace.

'I could arrange for a couple of the workers from the family estate to come down here and take care of the animals and tend to the plants during the day time. My maintenance man could come and look at your roof problem and fix your central heating for you. That would take a huge weight off your mind, wouldn't it?'

She made a vaguely dismissive movement. 'That's very kind of you to offer, but if I could afford to pay outside workers, I would have done it already. I'm just not that well off.'

'You won't have to pay them. I'm loaning them to you in return for your help at the hospital. We have a team of people with various skills on the estate, and I'm sure we can spare a couple to come over here to work for a while. Besides, it wouldn't necessarily need to be full time, would it?' He studied her closely, seeing the debate going on in her mind. 'And I'm pretty sure that the matron in charge would be able to find room for Becky to stay in the crèche while you're at work. Failing that, we could always take a look at the private nurseries.'

She raised a dark brow. 'And what about the fact that I like looking after Becky? Where does that come into your calculations?'

He had the grace to look uncomfortable at that, but he

gave it some deeper consideration. 'What about coming back to work part-time?' he suggested after a while. 'With a view to increasing the hours if it suited you?'

They had reached the duck pond by now, and Ruby stopped to look over at the ducks, who were skimming the surface of the water, dipping their beaks into the pond every now and again to capture a tasty morsel.

'See, their wings are drooping,' she murmured, pointing out a couple of birds that swam close to the reeds surrounding the pond. 'They don't look right to me. How will your workers know if something's wrong?'

'Because they're good at what they do, otherwise I wouldn't be employing them—and you're changing the subject,' Sam admonished her. 'The vet will sort out the livestock's problems, won't he? I need you to concentrate on how much happier you'll be when you're back in A&E where you belong.'

She smiled at that and swivelled around to face him. 'You're so sure that's the right thing to do, aren't you? Well, you needn't think it's going to be as easy as that to get me to accept what you say. I wouldn't even consider coming back unless it was on my terms.'

Now he looked less sure of himself. 'And those would be?'

'For a start you would have to agree to set on some more nurses. I'm not talking agency nurses, who can be expensive, I grant you. I mean speculate to accumulate, and give us extra staff so that we can cover all eventualities.'

He began to shake his head. 'I'm not sure that's possible. Management would probably object.'

'You are management,' she said. 'You're on the board, for heaven's sake. You can fix it.'

He moved his head in a 'maybe' sort of way. 'Is that it?' he asked. 'If I sort that out, would you consider coming back?'

'Certainly not.' She warmed to her theme. 'If I were to do

that, and I'm making no promises, I'd need your agreement that we would work together to make sure the unit had a good chance of survival…and I mean work together, not just you paying lip service to what I have to say. I had a notion that it would be a good idea to organise a charity fair to raise funds…and we would definitely have to do away with some of the more expensive outsourcing contracts. Bring more of the contractors into the employ of the hospital rather than using outsiders.'

'It sounds as though you're at least giving the idea some thought.'

'I'm giving it a fair consideration.'

He gave her a rueful smile. 'I'd almost go so far as to say you had a ready-made bargaining stance hidden up your sleeve. I wouldn't put it past you to have planned all this right from the start.'

'Now you've cut me to the quick.' She gave him what should have been an indignant frown, but she struggled to keep it up for very long. 'I'm hurt that you think I could be so devious.'

'I wouldn't want you to be hurt in any way,' he murmured, moving closer. 'I already feel bad that I took the job you wanted. Perhaps I should try to kiss you better,' he added softly, leaning towards her and allowing his lips to brush hers as though testing for a reaction.

She was too stunned by his actions to have time to put up any kind of resistance, and perhaps he read her lack of response as acquiescence because in the next moment he moved in on her, drawing her close and wrapping his arms around her. Then he kissed her firmly on her mouth.

It was a warm and vibrant experience, one that unexpectedly thrilled her to the core. She felt the aftershock of that kiss tingle along her nerve endings, sending small spirals of sweet sensation as far as her extremities, so that her pulses throbbed and her toes curled in delicious expectation.

It was a wonderful feeling being gathered up into his arms and soundly kissed, even as it was totally astonishing, and her whole body responded by going into complete meltdown. His kiss simply took her breath away.

Slowly, reluctantly, he dragged his mouth from hers, and she stared up at him in bemused wonder, her head reeling with a myriad of questions.

'Is something wrong?' he asked, looking down into her eyes and seeing her dazed expression.

'I…uh…I'm not exactly sure,' she murmured. 'What was that all about?'

His mouth made a rueful twist. 'It seemed like a good idea at the time,' he said. 'Have I blown my chances?'

'Chances of what?' she asked.

'That you'll come back to A&E.'

'Ah,' she said on a wavering sigh. 'A&E, of course.' Actually, she reflected, that was probably the best place for her right now because somehow her rational mind seemed to have detached itself from the rest of her body and was off floating somewhere in the ether. Was it going to be possible to put her back together again? 'I'll have to get back to you on that one.'

He frowned, shooting her a quizzical glance.

For her part, she decided it was just as well that he had let go of her because only then with some small space between them was she able to start functioning properly again. And her senses were telling her that they were no longer alone.

She glanced towards the farmhouse and saw that Craig, the vet, was coming into view, calling her name as he stepped onto the terrace at the back of the house.

'Over here,' she said, lifting a hand in acknowledgement. 'I'm over by the pond.'

Craig started towards her. Long and lanky, with dark hair and grey eyes, he had been a friend for as long as she could remember.

She sent Sam an oblique glance. 'I need to explain to him what's going on with the animals.'

Sam nodded. 'I'll leave you to it, then. Will you think about what I said?'

'I will.'

'Good. I'll be in touch in the next day or so if that's okay?'

'Okay.' By now Craig had reached them, but before she had time to make the introductions, the young vet had gathered her up in his arms and was hugging her fiercely. She was vaguely aware of Sam looking on with a frown.

'It's good to meet up with you again, Ruby,' Craig said. 'We don't get to see enough of you these days.' He drew back a little and looked into her eyes. 'I know how busy you are. Sophie's always telling me how hard you work.' Then he frowned. 'It's a real worry that she's disappeared, isn't it? You must let me help you in any way I can. Anything I can do, you know I'm here for you.' He draped an arm around her shoulders and turned to look expectantly at Sam.

For some reason, Sam's frown had deepened as he looked Craig over, and Ruby hastened to introduce the two men. 'Sam's taken over the A&E department,' she told the vet. 'He has to try to lick it into shape or risk it closing.'

Craig winced. 'I don't envy you that task,' he said, nodding towards Sam. He lightly squeezed Ruby's shoulder. 'I know how hard Ruby worked to keep things together for as long as she did. Her boss was retiring, so he didn't have too much of an input in that direction towards the end.'

Sam nodded. 'Everybody sings her praises.' He glanced towards her. 'I should go,' he said. 'I'll call you.' He inclined his head briefly towards both of them and then began to walk away, his long stride covering the ground in quick time.

Ruby sensed he was troubled, but whether that was because of the vet's arrival or because of her unwillingness to give him an answer to the work situation, she didn't know.

CHAPTER FIVE

'WE'RE not collecting so many eggs these days,' Ruby said, scattering a handful of grain on the rough ground where the hens were pecking for food. 'Gran says it's because the hens are getting on a bit.'

'That may be so, or it could be that you need to introduce new breeds to the farm.' Craig glanced around, watching the hens as they scratched in the dirt and hunted for food amongst the stones in the yard. It had been a few days since Ruby had first called him out, but now Craig was back on the smallholding to see if the animals were doing any better.

'Rhode Island Reds are not always the best choice for egg production these days,' he told her. 'You could try introducing other breeds, like Welsumer or Marans if you prefer brown eggs…Leghorns if you want white eggs.'

'Hmm. I'll give it some thought. It might actually be down to me to make the decision in the end because my grandparents are thinking of giving up the smallholding for good. They've found a lovely little retreat on the coast, and they offered me the chance to buy this place at a more than reasonable price, rather than let it go to strangers. I must say, I'm seriously tempted.'

Craig grinned. 'You're getting used to this way of life, aren't you? I could see it happening, even years ago when you came over here to visit in the summer holidays or whenever you had a weekend free. You've always loved the rural atmosphere, haven't you? It occurred to me that you had a dilemma years ago between choosing medicine or opting for life on the farm.'

'Well, medicine won in the end, didn't it? I suppose I thought saving lives would be more satisfying in the long run.'

'True. I wonder if you'd still be at the hospital if your new boss hadn't come along? He's not exactly a people person, is he? Strange that, in a doctor…but, then, I heard the odd snippet about him when I was at university. He comes from a boarding school background, by all accounts. His parents spent most of their time abroad, while he and his brother were looked after by relatives for a good part of the holidays. It doesn't really make for an all-round happy, integrated soul, that kind of upbringing, does it?'

Ruby frowned, thinking about that. 'No, possibly not. Are you saying that he studied at the same university as you?'

'Only for a short time. I just heard of him in passing, so to speak. He was the top student of his year. His family's fabulously wealthy—old money, and all that, going back through generation after generation.'

'I see.' Her brows lifted briefly in acknowledgement. 'That explains the country estate, I suppose.' She quickly shrugged off thoughts of Sam's origins. Thinking about him only reminded her of the way he'd kissed her, and that only served to make her unsettled and added to her indecision. It had been totally unexpected, given the kind of man he was.

'It's only now that Sophie has taken off that I've had a chance to rethink my options,' she said. 'Before she went, I was torn about what to do for the best, but now this whole way of life is beginning to grow on me once again.'

Despite the fact that Sam had offered her the chance to go back to work in A&E, Ruby had still not made up her mind what she ought to do. Becky took up a great deal of her time, and until the situation with Sophie was brought to a satisfactory conclusion, she simply couldn't settle to anything else. She was worried about what was happening to her sister, and each day Sophie stayed away her fears for her safety intensified. She'd told Sam she needed more time, and he'd had no choice but to accept that.

'I think you're a natural farmer,' Craig said, smiling. 'You sensed that something was wrong with the animals and took steps to put it right. It was only a question of changing the food mix and generally making them feel comfortable after their routine was changed, and things seem to be getting back to normal once more. Candy's looking his usual self again, and the ducks are none the worse for wear. They sometimes drop their feathers because they're getting too much protein in their diet, but we've done what we can to put that right. I'm sure everything will be fine before too long.'

'You're an eternal optimist,' Ruby said. 'You always were inclined that way.'

'Better that than the opposite,' Craig murmured. 'I like to think that Sophie will come back into our lives at any moment. Anything else is too worrying to contemplate.'

'Yes, you're right, though she did send me a brief text message, so I know that nothing terrible has happened to her. I just wish I knew where she was, so that I could go and bring her home.'

'At least you know she must be reasonably safe,' Craig commented. 'Did she give any clue as to what was wrong?'

Ruby shook her head. 'All she said was that she's sorry she had to leave and that she's missing Becky. I had the impression she felt she wasn't able to look after her properly because she was unwell. It's all so unsettling. It could be that she's going through a bad case of postnatal depression, but I tend to think there's more to it than that. I sent a message in return, begging her to come home, but there's been nothing since.'

She finished feeding the animals and then walked back with him towards the house. Becky was spending the day with her parents, which left her free for a while, and gave her a chance to catch her breath. These last few weeks it had felt as if her world was spinning out of control and she had been powerless to stop it.

'I'd better go on with my house calls,' Craig said, pausing to give her a goodbye hug. 'Keep your chin up. You're not on your own in this. Remember, I'm just a phone call away…and if you hear anything more of Sophie, let me know, won't you?'

'I will. Thanks, Craig.' She saw him out and then went back to the kitchen, where she looked around and contemplated the stack of chores that still needed to be done. She switched on the radio before setting about loading the washing machine, and the sound of a haunting melody filled the room. Somehow, it made her think of Sam, and perhaps that was because there was a brooding quality to the music, a restrained theme that reminded her of the way he held his thoughts close to his chest. It must have taken a lot for him to seek her out and ask her to come back. He wasn't the sort of man who would be comfortable showing any sign of vulnerability.

Some half an hour later, she was putting the finishing touches to her weekly magazine feature when snatches of the local news bulletin filtered through to her from the radio. 'Ambulances are being called out to a major accident on the motorway. It is feared that there are many casualties as a result of the incident, which occurred when a lorry collided with a camper van and crossed the central reservation. It is believed that several people are still trapped in their vehicles. Local hospitals have been put on standby.'

Ruby stopped what she was doing and felt a cold shiver run through her. This was bad. An accident of that kind meant that all the emergency units would be under pressure, and lives were at risk. How could she sit here and do nothing? It was unthinkable.

A few minutes later, after a brief phone conversation with the triage nurse on duty, she was on her way to the hospital.

'Ruby, thank heavens you're here,' Olivia greeted her. 'You don't know how much we've missed you. It's so good to have you back—though I wish it could have been under different circumstances.' The senior house officer was dressed in green scrubs, ready to receive the first of the casualties as they came in by ambulance.

Ruby nodded. 'Me too. I wish it didn't have to be this way, but I suppose things will never change. We'll always be needed here. I'll go and get ready.'

She changed in the locker room, emerging just as Sam was passing by on his way towards the ambulance bay.

'Hi there,' he said with a smile, lightly touching her arm and sending a surge of instant heat racing through her veins. 'It's great to have you here. Is Becky in the crèche?'

'No. She's with my parents for the day. When I heard the news of the accident, it was a question of whether to finish off my magazine article, gather in the last of the crop of raspberries…or come here. Not much of a choice, really.'

He smiled. 'It was a good decision. We're expecting at least a dozen injured people to arrive, including a young child—a five-year-old who was in the back seat of his parents' car. Would you take care of the boy? As far as we know, he suffered a chest trauma. He's still conscious, but he's complaining of chest pain, and he's having difficulty breathing and talking. There's a swelling in his throat, according to the paramedic who phoned in a report. His mother has shoulder and leg fractures, while the father has multiple injuries. James and I will supervise their treatment in the same resus room as the boy. There's also a little girl, two years old…but she came out of it unscathed, apparently.'

'That was something of a miracle, given what I've heard about the pile up,' she murmured. 'Of course I'll take care of the boy.'

'Good. Let's go, then. They should be arriving at any minute now.'

The boy was in a very bad way, she discovered, when the paramedics wheeled him into A&E a short time later. He was already turning blue from lack of oxygen, his breathing was noisy and laboured, and he was making moaning sounds.

'I'm going to intubate him,' Ruby told Michelle, who came to assist her. 'As soon as I have the tube in place in his throat, and we have him back on oxygen, we'll get a chest X-ray.'

She worked swiftly, securing the child's airway and examining him thoroughly to ensure that she missed nothing.

'Jason—my son—how is he?' his mother asked from the next bed. 'He couldn't breathe properly. He wasn't talking. What's happening to him?' The woman was in a lot of pain, but her thoughts were centred on her child and her husband. Beside her, still in her baby car seat, her two-year-old daughter was screaming loudly as a doctor tried to examine her.

'We're looking after him,' Ruby told her. 'I'm going to put a tube in his arm so that we can replace any fluids that he's losing. Be reassured that we're doing everything we can for him.'

She was desperately worried about this boy, who was failing fast, but nothing would be served by causing his mother more anxiety. She suspected that his condition was worsening because of internal bleeding, but the problem was in finding where the blood loss was coming from. As it was, his heart rate was sky high, his peripheral pulse was weak, and his breathing difficulties were increasing by the minute.

Michelle wheeled the portable X-ray machine into place, and Ruby checked the images on screen. 'There's a contusion to his lung,' she told the nurse, 'and air has leaked out from both lungs into the chest cavity. I'll put in drainage tubes to see if that will clear the problem.'

As soon as that was done, she left the boy in Michelle's care, under intense observation, and went to assist with the rest of the injured.

Sam was still working with the boy's father, and now he called for a trauma team to assist as the man went into cardiac arrest. His patient's injuries were severe, but up to now Sam had managed to deal with the various fractures he'd presented with, and he had done what he could to stop the bleeding. Now, though, the man's heart had given out under the strain.

Sam remained calm and efficient the whole time, doing his utmost to save the man's life, and using the defibrillator to shock his heart back into a normal rhythm. It didn't work.

'Asystole,' James said, checking the monitor, and Ruby was dismayed to see the flat line across the screen that showed no output from the heart.

The team was deflated. All their efforts were for nothing, and this man, who had a young wife and children, was unlikely to survive.

'Continue with the chest compressions,' Sam said tersely. 'Ruby, intubate him and put him on the ventilator. Olivia, we'll give him intravenous adrenaline. Check the monitor every two minutes. I need to figure out if he's bleeding internally.'

'An abdominal bleed?' Ruby asked, and he nodded.

'That's the most likely cause of his problems.'

They worked with him for the next few minutes, and then, just as they were beginning to think all was lost, the monitor bleeped. 'We have a rhythm,' Olivia said. 'He's back.'

There were smiles of relief all round, but Sam was on the move. 'I'm going to do an ultrasound scan of the abdomen to see if I can find the source of the bleeding. With any luck I can use an endoscope to seal the leaking blood vessel.'

Ruby would have liked to stay and help with that, but

Michelle came hurrying towards her from across the room. 'You need to take a look at little Jason. His vital signs are worsening.' Her expression was concerned, and Ruby realised that the situation was urgent.

'All right, let's get a CT scan,' Ruby said after examining the child once more. 'It's possible that he has a ruptured bronchus and that he's bleeding into his airways. We need to find out for sure.'

'That's very rare, isn't it—a rupture to the main branch of the airway?' Michelle frowned.

'Yes, it is, but it's something we need to check, all the same.'

Sam glanced at her. 'Are you going to be okay dealing with that?' he asked, and she nodded.

'If I have any problems, I'll call you,' she said, though he looked as if he had enough on his hands right now.

The CT scan confirmed her worst fears. 'We need to get him up to theatre,' she told Michelle. 'I'll do a thoracotomy—open up his chest and stop the bleeding that way, otherwise he has little or no chance of survival. You'll need to scrub in…and find me an anaesthetist, will you?'

A little more than an hour later, Ruby came out of the operating room, tossed her protective overgarments into the bin, cleaned up and went into the annexe. She was suddenly bone weary, the last of her adrenaline draining out of her, and she leaned back against the wall for a moment or two, sucking in air.

'Are you okay?' Sam said, walking into the room and coming to stand beside her. 'I came to see how you were doing. You're very pale.'

'I'm fine,' she told him. 'I don't usually react this way when we're under pressure, but somehow the thought of that small family being torn apart is beginning to get to me.'

'How is the boy?' His brows drew together as he watched her mouth flatten.

'He's on life support, and we need to get him into Intensive Care. I've done everything I can for him. I repaired a massive tear in the bronchus, and I'm hoping the chest drainage tubes will gradually ease the pressure in the chest cavity and elsewhere. Air has even collected under his skin, so that you can hear the crackles when you touch him. That poor child…'

'He was fortunate that he had you here to look after him.' Sam's voice was matter of fact, not allowing any shred of wasteful emotion. 'I doubt anyone else would have thought to look for a ruptured bronchus in such quick time. That's where skill and experience come into play.'

She sent him a weary look. 'That, and the fact that this A&E department is still in existence. Though that could end any time soon, couldn't it?' She sighed. 'How's his father bearing up? Did you find out the cause of his trouble?'

He nodded. 'There was a laceration in his liver. I managed to repair it. He should pull through all right, with any luck.'

She smiled at that. 'I don't think luck comes into it. You're a good surgeon, one of the best, from what I've seen and heard.' She straightened up. 'I really hope this family come out of this disaster safe and sound. I want to think of them having a future together, a wonderful family unit, sharing good times, supporting one another through all of life's ups and downs. That's what families are all about, isn't it?'

Her eyes misted a little as she thought back to her own past. 'I remember when I was Jason's age, we all went to spend a long weekend at the seaside. Sophie was two years old, like Jason's little sister, and she spent the days telling everyone who would listen that she was going to make a huge sandcastle on the beach and when it was finished she would decorate it to make it fit for a princess. Little as she was, she made everyone hunt along the water's edge for shells, and they had to be just right, the perfect shape and colour, or she would reject them.'

She might have expected him to smile at that, but his gaze was solemn, smoke grey, with a brooding quality that made her wonder what kind of experiences he'd had in life. He made no comment.

'She told me that she wanted to take Becky to that same place when she was a little older, and she was going to show her where she built the castle. She wanted her to have the same glorious memories that she did.'

'And yet she walked out on her daughter and left you to pick up the pieces. That doesn't say a great deal for the family spirit, does it?' He gave her that same no-nonsense look that he had given her before.

She sent him a long, thoughtful glance. He had such a practical, straightforward way of looking at things, and he was so dismissive of sentiment, of emotional ties. How could she begin to understand a man like him?

'It says that people have their ups and downs, and you need to stick together in order to get over them. I know that my sister loves her daughter, and that it must have taken something disastrous to make her stay away. It grieves me that I can't find her or do anything to help her.' She hesitated. 'You have a younger brother, don't you? Didn't you have good times together…or weren't there occasions when you helped each other out?'

'We enjoyed long breaks by the sea,' he said, 'sometimes with our parents, and other times with our grandparents.'

His expression sobered, a bleak quality coming into his eyes. 'As to helping each other out, it's probably best not to think too deeply about that. We had to rely on each other a good deal because we were at boarding school together for the major part of the year.'

He leaned back against the wall, his long legs crossed over at the ankles, his hands thrust into the pockets of his scrubs. 'My brother had a hard time settling, and since I had been there for a couple of years before him, I did what I could to make him feel that he wasn't alone. Up until then he'd been with our grandparents.'

He looked at her, sensing her frown. 'It wasn't that our parents wanted to leave us...it was more that they had the pressure of international business interests swamping them. Alongside that, they were trying to bring medical facilities to countries that wouldn't otherwise have the benefit. Who am I to argue with that kind of altruism?'

'But they did it at the expense of their children's happiness, didn't they?'

'I don't see it that way, and nor did they. They wanted us to have a good education, the best, and they succeeded in that. We both went on to carve out satisfying careers for ourselves. My brother has done well. He set up his own financial consultancy in Scotland. His wife works with him, and his boys enjoy living in a beautiful house surrounded by moorland and lochs.'

'It sounds idyllic.' She slanted him a questioning glance. 'Didn't you ever feel that you wanted to have that kind of life for yourself?'

'With a wife and family, you mean?' He shook his head. 'It isn't something I've ever really thought about—or wanted, for that matter. I don't have time for that sort of commitment, or any long-term, all-or-nothing kind of relationship with strings attached. I know it's not easy for any woman to settle for what I would be prepared to offer, but that's how it is. I have too much still to do getting to where I want to be.'

He looked around. 'This is just the start—I want to be there in the setting up of state-of-the-art units. It means everything to me to see to it that people have the best care we can give them...and that includes keeping this place going. It doesn't have to be new, just working at full capacity, bringing the best we have in people and resources to serve the local area.'

She gave a wry smile. 'And there's no room in all that for meaningful relationships?' It seemed strange to her that he could rule out the prospect of finding and appreciating enduring love. 'Don't you feel you're missing out in some way?'

His dark brows shot up. 'I'm not missing out. What makes you think that?' He straightened up, moving to face her, closing in and winding an arm around her waist. 'I'm here with you,' he said softly, 'and that has to be good, doesn't it? You're beautiful, lovely to hold…and alongside all that you have a glorious, laid-back attitude to life, and you're not afraid to speak your mind.' His mouth curved, his long body shielding hers, blocking her escape by the simple means of an outstretched arm, palm flat against the wall at the side of her neck. 'How much better could it be?'

'Um…I should tell you,' she said, gazing up at him and feeling the lure of those eyes that were blue-grey like the depths of the ocean, 'that from the sound of it, I'm really not your type. I'm an all-or-nothing kind of girl. I wouldn't like you to get the wrong idea.'

'I won't,' he murmured, his head lowering, his lips moving ever closer to hers. 'I'm just glad that you came here today.'

By now his lips had settled on hers, nudging them softly so that they parted in a gentle sigh of delicious response, and the heart-melting kiss that followed took her breath away. He captivated her with his sensuous demand, drawing from her every drop of sweet, feverish yearning that was pent up inside her.

How was it that he could make her feel this way? The question came to her through the mists of warm, heady sensation. They had nothing in common except for a deep, abiding sense of commitment to their patients. Even in that she had fallen by the wayside, but it was as if none of that mattered now. All she cared about was that he was kissing her, and her entire body was on fire, the blood pulsing through her veins in ecstatic, hectic response.

She couldn't think straight any more. His hands stroked along the length of her spine, drawing her to him, so that her breasts were crushed against the solid wall of his chest, and she felt the thunder of her heartbeat so strongly that she felt sure he must feel it too. He bent his head and began to nuzzle the delicate column of her throat.

She ran her hand lightly over his rib cage, expecting to feel the fine linen of his shirt, and encountered instead the thin cotton of his scrubs. A faint sense of shock ran through her. Scrubs meant that they were in the hospital…how could she have forgotten that?

Through the thin material, she absorbed the warmth of his skin, and everything in her wanted to lean in closer, to revel in the sheer heaven of being in his arms…only by now reality had stepped in, reminding her of where they were…and of what he had said. He didn't believe in long-term relationships, and from her point of view it would be madness to even think about getting involved with any man right now. She'd been hurt once before, and why would she want to set herself up for more unhappiness?

Her palm flattened, gently pushing against his chest, and at the same time she shifted a little, moving out of reach of his seeking mouth.

He looked at her, his eyes still smoky with passion, but he registered her withdrawal and gazed at her questioningly.

'I can't do this,' she said.

He took a slow step away from her, giving her breathing space, and she stayed very still for a moment, allowing herself time to think.

'I'm sorry,' he said. 'I didn't mean to step out of line. I don't know what came over me. It's just that from the moment you walked into A&E this morning, it felt as though the world was putting itself right. It's odd, I know. But it feels good having you around, and whenever you're near me, lately, I get this urge to kiss you and hold you.'

She gave a rueful smile. 'Perhaps you should try to overcome it,' she said. 'Like I said, I'm an old-fashioned kind of woman. I may hanker after the warmth and delight of a wonderful relationship and all that goes along with it, but I also want love and commitment, and I don't think I'm prepared to give up on that dream. Not that you were offering any of that, of course…but just so that you know…I have enough to deal with right now. I'm not sure I'm ready for any of this.' Her life was chaotic as she juggled so many different roles. How could she even think of getting tangled up in a relationship with a man who admitted his career took precedence over everything?

'Of course. I'm totally out of order.' He pressed his lips together in an expression of regret. 'I don't usually behave like this, you know…but then again, I've never met a woman quite like you before.'

'You haven't?' She wasn't at all sure whether she could believe him. Didn't all the women who had fallen for him in the past believe that they were the one and only woman for him? What good had it done them when he had eventually moved on?

He shook his head. 'You're one of a kind, Ruby. Which makes me all the more keen not to upset you in any way.'

He took another step backwards, emphasising his point by his actions, and then studied her intently. 'Would you give some more thought to coming back to work on a formal basis?'

She marvelled at the way he morphed smoothly into business mode, but didn't that just go to show how accomplished he was at separating his emotions from his physical desires?

'I've already made arrangements to set on a couple of nurses,' he said, 'and I'm having meetings with the maintenance contractors to see if we can sort out some different kind of set up.'

She raised her brows. 'You are?'

He nodded. 'And that's not all. I've worked out a plan

for making huge savings on the drugs bill for the whole of the hospital.'

She sent him a cautious glance. 'Isn't that a bit risky? Surely we need all the medicines that we currently use—not only that, we should be certain that we have the right quality of drug.'

'That's true in all respects. But I've spoken to the board members about it, and they've agreed that we will arrange for competing suppliers to bid for our custom in an online auction. That way we bring in offers of lower prices—we've already tested it out, and the savings will be tremendous.'

'You have been busy,' she said. 'I can see you're a force to be reckoned with. No wonder the board set you on.'

He gave a short laugh. 'You're never going to forgive me for that, are you?'

Ruby shrugged. 'I'm getting there,' she said. 'Slowly.'

He tilted his head slightly to one side. 'So does that mean you'll come back? We really need you here working alongside us.'

She thought about it. This morning's events had shown her just how important her work was to her, and surely it would be madness to give it up? The fact that she had done every-thing she could to save that little boy's life meant more to her than anything. Besides, putting all other more professional and philanthropic considerations to one side, she had come to realise that if she wanted to buy the farm off her grandpar-ents, the money would definitely come in handy.

'I suppose I'll have to come back,' she murmured, 'or you'll be forever nagging me, won't you?'

He gave her a beaming smile and draped an arm around her shoulders. 'Now, would I do that?' he asked.

'Oh yes,' she said as they started to walk towards the lift that would take them back down to A&E. 'I'm becoming quite convinced you'll stop at nothing to get your own way.'

'I'm wounded you should think so,' he murmured, 'but

since we're on the subject, I've been trying to work out how I can persuade you to come over to visit my family estate at the weekend.'

She blinked. 'I thought we just had a conversation about you mending your ways?'

'So we did…but this is work related, you see. I've arranged to hold a fund-raising event in aid of the A&E department, and I think I need some input from you—it being your idea in the first place, of course.'

She sent him a narrowed glance. 'Why is it I get the feeling you're railroading me into doing things I wouldn't normally contemplate?'

'I can't begin to imagine the reason,' he said, assuming an air of innocence. 'Beats me.'

CHAPTER SIX

'IF anybody needs me, I'll be over in Intensive Care, checking up on young Jason. It's been a couple of days since he was brought in, and I want to see how he's doing.' Ruby added her signature to the patient's chart and handed it to Michelle. 'Everything's reasonably under control here, so I'm going to slip away while I have the chance to grab a few minutes. I've sent Olivia to the staff lounge to take a well-earned break, but James is around if anything should crop up. I've no idea where Sam is this morning, but you can page either of us if there's a problem.'

'Will do.' Michelle quickly ran her gaze over the pre-scribed medication outlined on the chart and then lifted her head to look back at Ruby, her silky black hair swinging lightly with the motion. 'That's the thing about Sam, isn't it? He's always busy, either with patients or in admin, but he never bothers to tell anyone what he's doing. He's a worka-holic, forever on the move.'

The nurse placed the chart at the end of their young patient's bed. 'I used to think he didn't care much for mixing with staff, but it isn't that at all…he's fine when you do manage to collar him…it's just that he always seems to have a thousand and one things to do and doesn't feel it necessary to explain himself to anyone.'

'He's a complicated man, that's for sure,' Ruby said as they walked towards the central desk, 'but he appears to be coping well under a lot of pressure. He has a lot of new systems to put in place if we're to avoid closure, and they're taking up a lot of his time. Eventually, when things settle down, I expect he'll be more available, but in the meantime the trainees will have to come to me, or page him if they find they are having difficulties.'

'I'm sure that's what he expects them to do. If there's a problem, he wants the junior doctors to come and find him, or sometimes he'll already have stepped in and be there dealing with it…and he doesn't see the point in making a fuss over anything. He just believes in getting on with the job.'

'That's true, though he ought to stop and take a few minutes for himself every now and again. It doesn't do anyone any good to work at full pelt the whole time.' Ruby had her suspicions that Sam had an inbuilt 'on' switch, and that he didn't have it in him to wind down. This constant busy, busy, busy attitude drove her to distraction.

She hurried to Intensive Care, which was along the corridor from the A&E department, and spent a few minutes there talking to the sister in charge.

'All being well, we'll take Jason off the ventilator later on today,' the nurse told her. 'The consultant wants to make sure first of all that there have been no setbacks overnight, but from what we've observed he's still making good progress. He's looking altogether much better now, and his heart rhythm and respiration have both improved. The drainage tubes will most likely stay in place for another twenty-four hours, though. We have him on antibiotics because of the risk of infection, but all in all he seems to be going along very well.'

'That's brilliant news, Jen.' Ruby smiled at her. 'I'll go and take a peek at him, if I may?'

'Of course. He's still under sedation, so he won't know

much about what's going on, but his mother's been sitting with him a lot of the time. She isn't here at the moment because the doctor on her ward wants to check her over, but the nurses bring her here from women's surgical each day.'

'I thought they might. What about his father? Is there any news of him?'

'He's in the adult intensive care unit. Last I heard, he was still experiencing some abnormal heart rhythms, but, considering the injuries he received, that's not really surprising. It'll take a while for him to heal.'

Ruby nodded and a few moments later went to stand by the boy's bed, looking at the monitors that registered his heart rate, respiration and temperature, along with blood oxygen levels.

The child appeared to be sleeping peacefully, his brown hair spiky against the white of the pillow, and someone had placed a teddy bear against the side bars of his bed, so that it would be the first thing he saw when he woke up. He was still pale, but there was faint colour in his cheeks, and he looked to be in a much better state than he had when she had last seen him.

'Thanks for letting me look in on him, Jen,' she told the nurse as she was about to leave. 'I feel much happier for knowing that he's doing all right.'

'You're welcome, any time.'

Ruby made her way back to A&E feeling much lighter in spirit. Some things, at least, seemed to be going along well enough. Now all she needed was for her sister to come back home and repair the broken bond with her baby daughter.

'I've been looking for you,' Sam said, meeting up with her in the corridor as she was about to go back to work. There was a hint of exasperation in his voice. 'I wanted to talk to you about one of your patients—a girl who fell off her bike—but I couldn't find you anywhere in A&E.'

'That's because I was in ICU, checking up on my thoracotomy patient.'

He frowned. 'The little boy? But you treated him two days ago, didn't you? He's not our patient any more.'

'Maybe not, but I wanted to know how he was doing.'

'Couldn't you have given the unit a ring to find out how he was?'

'I could, but it wouldn't have been the same. I preferred to go and look in on him.'

'Whatever for?'

She stared at him, raising her brows in an expression of astonishment. 'Do you really need to ask?'

'Yes, I think I do. What is it with all this touchy-feely stuff that goes on around here? You treat the patients, you do what you can for them, and then you need to move on. There are always other people waiting to be seen.'

'That might be your way of doing the job,' she said, tapping the security code into the main door of the A&E unit, 'but it isn't mine. I do what I can to make sure that I stabilise the patients who are brought in here as emergencies, but when I have a free moment, I like to follow up on them.' She pushed open the door and walked into the department, leaving him to trail in her wake. 'And I'm sure, if you give it a little more thought, you'll realise that you're misguided somewhere along the line. We do this job because we care. We're dealing with people, children and individuals, not numbers or statistics that make up targets to be met.'

She sent him a sharp glance. 'And while I'm on the subject, if you think you'll get me to change my ways, you're very much mistaken. If I wanted to become another version of you, I'd have taken a course in robotics or virtual medicine.'

Now it was his turn to raise his brows. 'I'm shocked. Whatever did I do to merit that tongue-lashing? All I'm saying is that if you get too involved with your patients, you'll come shuddering to a stop when anything bad happens to them, and then you won't be fit for anything. It doesn't do to have all this deep compassion and empathy for everyone you come into contact with.'

Her gaze narrowed on him. 'I think you should stop digging yourself deeper in the mire while you still have the chance to escape. I don't much care what your opinion is on the matter. I'll do as I think fit.' She made a brief, falsely sweet smile. 'Now, what was it you wanted to ask about the girl who fell off the bike? Much as I felt compassionate about what happened to her, I didn't offer to have the bike fixed. I simply treated her for a dislocated elbow and arranged for follow-up care.'

His mouth turned down at the corners in a crooked grimace. 'Sarcasm doesn't become you at all, Ruby. I thought you were above all that. I was just interested to know if you'd found any other injuries or problems when you examined her—only, her mother was asking about her being feverish. She told me she thought that might have led to the fall.'

'There was no fever. I checked the girl's temperature and asked about dizziness or faintness, but when she was alone with me briefly, the child said she came off the bike when she swerved to avoid her young brother, who ran into her path. I have the *feeling* that she didn't want to get him into trouble, so she invented a story about being headachy…if I'm allowed to use the word *feeling*, that is?'

'All right, all right. You win.' He put up his hands in submission. 'Let's call a truce, shall we?'

She gave a soft laugh and walked over to the central desk, where she began to check on new arrivals. Sam went to the computer and started to access information.

'There's a baby who needs to be seen right away,' the desk clerk said. 'He has a nasty case of diarrhoea, and the family doctor sent him here.'

'I'll go and look at him.' Ruby took the baby's chart from the rack and checked the details the triage nurse had written down. As she looked up, she saw a familiar figure coming towards her, a man that she had treated some time ago.

'Hello there,' Nick Dryden said. 'Remember me? You treated me a few weeks ago, and I had to go to the operating theatre to have my spleen removed.'

'Oh…yes, that's right.' Ruby gave him a quick glance. 'How are things with you? You're not here because you've done some more damage to yourself, are you?'

'No, nothing like that.' He smiled, his thin face lighting up a fraction. 'I had to come into the hospital for my check-up with the consultant, and I thought while I'm here I would see if you were around. I just wanted to say thanks for what you did, for listening to me. The nurse said it would be all right to come and find you.'

'I was glad to help,' Ruby told him. 'I hope things are going well for you.'

He nodded. 'Actually, it occurred to me that I must have seen you here before that day. It was when I came about the pain in my back one time. You didn't treat me, but I remember you because you were talking to a young woman over by the desk. She was having some problem with her hair, and you fixed a clip for her.'

Ruby frowned, thinking back. 'Oh, yes, that was probably my sister. She came to see me at work one day…I think she'd caught her hair clip on something, and she was in a bit of a tangle.'

Sophie had been for her first post-natal check that day, she recalled, while their mother was looking after Becky.

Beside her, Sam made a restless movement, and Ruby collected her thoughts. Too much touchy-feely interchange going on, was there? Sam was clearly restless and on fighting form today. He had achieved his objective of bringing her back into work, and now he wanted things to move smoothly on, without interruption.

'Well, it's good to see that you're feeling better,' she told the man. 'I can't stop and chat, I'm afraid…I have to go and see another patient.'

'That's okay. I understand.' He gave a slight waving motion with his hand and started to walk away.

The baby, who was a little younger than Becky, was suffering from a nasty tummy upset, Ruby discovered when she carefully examined him. Not only that but he was lethargic, with parched and cracked mucous membranes, had a very fast heart rate, and his breathing was disturbed.

'It looks as though the diarrhoea has caused him to become dehydrated,' she gently told the baby's mother. 'His fontanelle, this soft spot on the top of his head, is sunken, and he generally appears to be quite poorly.'

'I've tried to get him to drink,' the mother said, 'but he keeps vomiting; he can't keep anything down. That's why I took him to my doctor, but he said to bring him here.'

Ruby nodded. 'I'll do some tests to find out if it's a bug that we can treat with antibiotics, but usually these things are caused by a virus, and so that kind of treatment won't be of much use. What we'll do is admit him, and I'll make sure he gets fluids and the correct balance of rehydration salts through an intravenous line.'

'Thank you.' The woman seemed to relax a little. 'How long will he need to stay in hospital—do you know?'

'It could be a few days. Children usually respond very well to the treatment.' Ruby smiled at her. 'I'll leave you to talk to the nurse, and she will be able to explain anything you want to know and make any arrangements for you to be with your baby on our children's ward.'

The woman inclined her head in acknowledgement and cuddled her baby to her while Ruby made preparations to set up the drip.

Some time later, when she had seen to it that the infant was settled and the treatment started, Ruby made her way back to the main area of A&E. Sam was there, arranging for a cardiac specialist to come and see one of his patients, but as soon as he finished dealing with that, he came over to her.

'I was hoping we might get together some time to discuss plans for the fund-raiser,' he said. 'How are you fixed?'

'Oh…I'm glad you're going ahead with that.' She glanced at her watch. 'How about we do it now? I haven't taken a proper lunch break yet, so I dare say we could go and have something to eat and talk it through. Or were you about to go off duty? You have to go over to the Heritage this afternoon, don't you?'

'That's right, I do.' He gave her a fleeting, assessing glance. 'There's not much that escapes you, is there?'

'Not a great deal. It's all part of the job.' She smiled at him. 'So what shall we do? I know you're always in a hurry, but even you have to eat sometimes.'

He gently cupped her elbow with his hand and turned her towards the door. 'We'll go and eat,' he said. 'You can tell me how things are working out for you with young Becky.'

'Oh, she's not doing too badly,' Ruby told him. 'She had another tooth come through, so she's a little more settled now that's over and done with. Of course, she's missing her mum, and that's a bit upsetting. She looks around for her every now and again, as though she knows something precious is missing, and then there are times when she's fractious for no apparent reason…mainly when she's tired.'

They left the department and headed towards the hospital restaurant. 'You seem to be coping well enough,' he commented. 'Is she being looked after in the crèche at the moment?'

She shook her head. 'My mother is looking after her today.' Her mouth curved. 'She likes to get in her granny time when she can—lots of cuddles and masses of spoiling.'

He looked at her oddly, and she tilted her head to one side, looking at him and trying to fathom his reaction. 'Do you not find that your parents are the same with your brother's children,' she asked, 'or even that your grandparents were like that with you when you were small? You said that they looked after your brother for a while, didn't you, so I imagine they must have cared for you as well?'

He shrugged. 'It was a long time ago, and generally my grandparents lived some distance away from the family home. I don't see a lot of them, even now, though we get together for family occasions. As to my brother, he lives up in Scotland, so my parents go to see him whenever they can, but of course they're away a lot.'

'I can't imagine that kind of lifestyle,' she said. 'My family have always been reasonably close by, and we're always in touch one way or another. My grandparents are moving to live near the coast, but they won't be too far away even then…an hour or so by car. We often spend weekends together as a family, and I can't see that changing.'

They walked into the restaurant, and Sam picked up a couple of trays, handing one to her. 'It has still been a problem for you with Becky, though, hasn't it, even with close family to help. How have they all reacted to Sophie's disappearance?'

She winced. 'They're very worried. They tend to think that she was ill as a result of her pregnancy, and maybe because of the shock of discovering that Becky's father wasn't going to be around for her. They want to support her in any way they can, and both my parents and grandparents have suggested that she might go to live with them once she comes home.'

She grimaced faintly. 'I think Sophie felt that she ought to be able to manage on her own, but of course it didn't work out. Now all we can do is hope that we manage to find her. I think the police tend to take the view that she's an adult who made her own decision to leave. They suggested we involve social services to take care of Becky, but we declined that offer.'

Sam asked the woman behind the counter to add meat pie, potatoes and vegetables to his plate. 'Sophie lived with you for a time, didn't she?' he said, throwing Ruby a sideways glance. 'Was that your own house, or were you renting?'

'It was mine. I can't make up my mind whether to let it out or put it up for sale. I think I'm waiting to find out what happens with Sophie first of all, in case she comes back and needs to find a place of her own.'

She chose beef and vegetable casserole for her own lunch and added a cup of tea and a dessert of fruit and ice cream.

Sam was frowning as they went to find a table by the window. 'So you're definitely thinking of moving into your grandparents' place, then? I thought perhaps you might find it a bit too much to handle, now that you've decided to come back to work.'

'I didn't realise that you knew about that.' She sat down at the table and took a sip from her tea.

He made a half smile. 'I know the general consensus is that I don't mix too well or have any idea of what's going on, apart from on the work front, but I do tend to absorb all the chatter that goes on around me. Just because I don't always join in, it doesn't mean I don't know what's happening.'

'Ah…so you do have an idea about what people are thinking? They would really like for you to open up to them a bit more, you know.'

'Yes, well, maybe I will, as soon as I've manoeuvred the department into its new, lean, less costly shape.' He lifted his fork and slid it into a mound of creamy potato. 'So, how are you planning to make things work if you take over your grand-parents' place?'

'That,' she answered, scooping up a forkful of succulent vegetables, 'is what I still have to work out. It's just that the opportunity was too good to miss, and it's a beautiful old house, rambling, large, full of light, and with masses of land where children can run and play…so it would be good for the future—if ever I get as far as having a husband and children, that is.'

He sent her a thoughtful look. 'How would you feel if your prospective husband doesn't share your love of the place?'

Her brows drew together, and she wavered for a moment, her fork poised in the air as she pondered that. 'He'd obviously be the wrong man for me. What's not to like about that lovely farmhouse?'

She grinned. 'Of course, coming from your background, you'd probably find lots that was unsuitable…all that clutter and mess. Even the stream and the pond are haphazard and meandering, and as to the meadows—all those broken-down fences and ancient stiles must offend your sense of order. The trees are old and gnarled, and the apple orchard tends to be filled with fallen fruit in the autumn. I expect your country estate is all manicured lawns and neat gravelled drives, with not a weed to be seen anywhere.'

He raised a dark brow. 'Weeds? With all those gardeners employed to tend to the grounds week in and week out, I should think not.' His mouth made a crooked shape, and soft light glimmered in his eyes. 'Anyway, the house is a charming example of fine Georgian architecture, beautifully symmetrical in style, and it has certainly stood the test of time. I'm really quite taken with it. It isn't mine, of course, though it has been in the family for generations.'

'No. I understand that.' She frowned. 'Have you never thought of getting a place of your own?'

He gave a negligent shrug. 'Not really. Up to now I've usually rented apartments because I've been on the move, going wherever promotion took me. I suppose now that I'm on the board of the hospitals trust, I ought to consider finding somewhere, but it seems a waste when my parents are away so much and I already have a wing to myself in the family home.'

'Will your parents object to you setting up a fund-raising event on the estate? That is what you plan to do, isn't it?'

'That's right. No, I don't see them having a problem with that. The grounds are extensive enough for us to take over one of the fields, maybe a second one for the car parking, and we should be able to provide everything we want within that area.'

'What did you have in mind?'

'Well, that's the question.' He leaned back in his chair and gestured with his hands to show a wide-open expanse. 'I'm open to suggestions. I thought a few stalls—cakes, bric-a-brac, plants and a raffle. Maybe some horse riding experiences for the youngsters…I haven't really thought much beyond that.'

She finished off her last forkful of carrots and sent him a questioning look. 'Where would you find the horses?'

'In our stables. We have several thoroughbreds that run regularly on the racing circuits, and there are grooms to attend to them, but we also have other horses that are gentle enough for untrained riders.'

She raised her eyes heavenward. 'It's another world out there, isn't it? How on earth did you ever come into medicine with that background?'

He chuckled. 'I think I was impressed by the medical profession from an early age. My parents set up facilities abroad, and sometimes they took me with them, so I was able to see how they were progressing. I was very taken with how people valued the chance to receive medical help, and I was touched by how much difference a doctor's intervention could make in someone's life. The actual decision to take up medicine as a profession, though, came while I was away at school.'

'You put me to shame,' she said. 'My medical career had quite mundane beginnings. I stuck plasters on my dolls and bandaged up my teddy bears, and they always miraculously recovered from whatever ailed them, so I was convinced from a very young age that I had the healing touch.'

He laughed. 'And I'm sure you do. You're very good at your job.'

'Thanks. I just hope we can keep this department going so that I still have a job to come to in a few months' time.' She drew the dish of fruit towards her and picked up her spoon. 'So what are we going to do about this fund-raiser? I suppose we could have a dog show. Those sorts of things tend to bring in a good crowd, don't they? Unless you have any objections to something like that?'

'Not at all. And, thinking about events that people can watch, I could ask the local tae kwon do team if they'd like to do an exhibition. They would be glad to take part, I think, to drum up support for their club and gain new members.'

'There you are…we've practically sorted it, haven't we? Shall I print out some posters? We could ask for volunteers at the village institute.'

'Yes, that would be good.' He began to eat his pudding, a stodgy treacle sponge that made her feel full up just looking at it.

'Do you want a taste?' he asked, picking up a fork and getting ready to offer her a sample.

'Uh…no thanks,' she murmured hastily. 'I'm fine with what I have. In fact, I'm already wondering if I haven't overdone it. My waistband feels as though it's expanded a couple of inches.'

'I'm sure that won't matter at all,' he said, his gaze travelling over her in appreciation. 'You look gorgeous: all soft, womanly curves, enough to make a man's pulse shoot into orbit. It's just as well that you're a paediatrician because if you were to give your tender loving care to the adult males who are brought in here, they'd probably keel over from their hearts going into overdrive.'

'Oh,' she said, looking at him in astonishment, her lips parting a fraction.

He groaned. 'Please don't look at me like that. It's diffi-cult enough to keep my distance as it is, but when you give me that wide-eyed look, it pushes everything else out of my head and just makes me want to kiss you. That's not good at all, not when I have to go back to work and concentrate on the job in hand.'

'Oh,' she said again, her eyes growing even wider, so that he pushed his dish away and got to his feet.

'If you've finished,' he murmured, 'perhaps we should go before things run out of control. I need to collect some files, and then I have to drive over to the Heritage and do my stint there.'

He held out a hand to her, and she slid her palm into his, allowing him to draw her to her feet. His grasp was warm and firm, and it was just as well that he was holding her because for a moment or two the world seemed to be out of kilter, and she had no idea why she was experiencing such a heady rush of heat from her toes to her face. She was sure her cheeks must be burning, and all she wanted right then was to get out of there, away from the restaurant and prying eyes.

Not that anyone would have noticed, she realised as she went with him out into the corridor. They were all far too busy refuelling themselves after a busy morning, and any feelings of embarrassment were entirely her own.

She walked with him back to A&E, and all the time he retained his hold on her hand, and she did nothing whatever to change that. He keyed the security code into the door panel and ushered her into the unit, draping his free arm around her waist, as though he knew she might crumple to the floor if he was to let go of her.

'Okay, then,' he murmured. 'I'll go and find those files.' They reached the door of his office, and he hesitated for a moment, pushing the door open and glancing at her as though he was going to invite her in.

'Yes, of course.' She looked at him, all too conscious of his palm still resting in the small of her back, aware of the subtle pressure that was gently coaxing her to come and join him.

'I should go back to work,' she said, and he gazed at her for a second or two, reading her indecision, and waiting hopefully for her to give in to his tender persuasion.

Instead, she took a small step backwards, and he reluctantly let his arm fall to his side, allowing her to go. Released, she finally began to breathe more easily. It would not have done for her to take him up on that unspoken invitation. She was far from immune to his masculine vibes, and just being near him was playing havoc with her senses. How did he manage to do this to her, to make her feel as though her whole body was yearning to have him hold her close?

She turned and walked away from him, pulling in a slow, deep breath, trying desperately to get herself together once more.

'Are you all right?' Michelle asked, her gaze following her as Ruby went to rummage through the stack of lab reports at the desk.

Ruby nodded. 'Of course. Why do you ask?'

'I saw you coming back from lunch,' the nurse said. 'You looked as though you'd been hit by the aftershock from a quake.'

'Did I?' Ruby blinked. 'We don't get those around here, do we?'

Michelle gave a short laugh. 'We do if Sam Boyd is around. I think it's known in some circles as the Boyd effect. Women have been known to fall for him, big time, according to the gossip in the nurses' quarters, but it never pays to think that you'll be the one to crack the code. They say he always moves on, especially if things start getting too serious.'

'Do they?' Even as she asked the question, Ruby had to accept that she knew it was true. Hadn't Sam told her as much himself? He had warned her that he didn't have time for commitment, for long-term relationships with strings attached, and perhaps there was more behind that than simply a desire to put all his energy into his chosen career. Maybe he was afraid of becoming emotionally involved. Why else would he steer clear of any deep and lasting attachment? 'Are some of the nurses suffering from broken hearts?'

'Not as far as I can tell, but you know how these things are bandied about. There are people who know people…and then the rumours start.'

'Well, thanks for telling me, but I wasn't actually planning on getting involved.'

'Maybe not.' Michelle's expression became serious. 'But it happens sometimes, and I wouldn't like to see you get hurt.'

Ruby sent her a quick, rueful smile. 'Thanks, Michelle, but I'm sure you're worrying unnecessarily. I don't have the time or energy for romance right now. I have enough on my plate at the moment with all the worry about my sister and having to look after Becky while at the same time trying to hold down a job. Besides, Sam and I have nothing whatever in common.' She went back to studying the lab reports.

It was true what she'd said, wasn't it? Sam was attracted to her, and he was more than ready to explore the various places where that could lead, but he lived in a different world from Ruby, and even if she'd been tempted by the lure of his sensual magnetism, she was far too sensible to allow herself to be pulled into his force field, wasn't she?

CHAPTER SEVEN

'WHY can't people take the time and trouble to refill the coffee pot when they see it's running empty?' Ruby said grumpily as she contemplated the dregs of coffee grounds in the filter. She picked up the filter paper and tossed it into the nearby bin.

The staff lounge was empty right now, except for herself and Sam, because there had been an influx of patients in A&E, and everyone was working at full tilt. Ruby had already been on duty for several hours, dealing with the usual crop of accidental injuries, respiratory difficulties and acute illness that brought people here during the weekend. Now, as this Saturday afternoon wore on, they were dealing with the aftermath of all-day drinking and injuries from fights that had broken out. The waiting room was full to overflowing, and there were a number of intoxicated, garrulous people waiting to be seen.

'Because it takes time and trouble, I would guess,' Sam said, throwing her a quick, assessing glance. 'What's wrong? You're not yourself today, are you? I've noticed you've had a tendency to be quite short-tempered at times. Is it the drunks taking over A&E? Are they beginning to get to you?'

Ruby shook her head. 'I'm used to them by now.' She put fresh coffee into a new filter, filled the jug with water and set it on the base to heat. 'I'm just tired because Becky had a bad night. I think she caught sight of one of her mother's sweaters when I was sorting through the wardrobe, and it must have triggered something in her mind. After that she was inconsolable. Nothing I did would put matters right.'

She sighed. 'And she's teething again, so that didn't help. She kept waking up and putting a finger in her mouth, and then she would start to sob and dribble, and it was just too awful. I ended up nursing her in my arms each time until she fell asleep. I didn't know what to do. I tried teething gel. I tried a nice bottle of warm milk, but she was very fractious.'

She made a brief grimace. 'Of course, this morning, when I took her over to my mother's house to be looked after, she was sleeping serenely like a little angel.' She pulled down a cup from the rack and sent him a taut glance. 'So all in all I'm not in the best of moods. Be warned.'

He pressed his lips together to hide a smile. 'What you need is doughnuts,' he murmured. 'Didn't you once tell me that they were the very thing that would put a smile on the face of everyone here?' He walked over to the fridge and drew out a box. Then he held it out to her. 'Here you are. Help yourself to something delicious.'

She lifted the lid and stared down at an assortment of doughnuts and cream cakes. 'Oh, bliss. Oh, joy,' she said. She looked up at him. 'Where did these come from? I mean, who brought them?'

'I did.' He smiled. 'Haven't you noticed that the snack trolley has been filled with goodies every day? I thought you were giving out extremely good advice, so I decided to act on it. And today, since it's the weekend, I reckoned we all needed an extra boost.'

'Mmm. I think I could kiss you,' she said, glancing up at him and taking a bun from the selection. 'I'm in more of an iced bun kind of a mood today, I think.' She bit into it, savoured the sweet flavours, licking the cream from her lips, and then looked at him with deep affection. 'I'm pretty sure you're my favourite person in all the world,' she murmured. She took another bite and then nodded. 'Yes, I'm sure of it. I'm in love, definitely.'

'With me or the bun?' He laughed and went over to the coffee machine. 'Sit down and I'll pour your coffee,' he said. 'Relish it for as long as you can because, as we both know, it's hell out there.'

She sat down and scoffed the rest of the bun while he made coffee and came to put a cup down on the table beside her. He waited until she had finished eating, watching in fascination as she licked her fingers clean slowly, one by one, and then he leaned over and planted a kiss firmly on her mouth.

'Mmm,' he said, drawing back eventually. 'Delightful. Sweet as sugar and absolutely delicious, you taste like perfection to me, grumpy or not.'

She stared up at him, a dazed look coming over her face, her senses dazzled by the swiftness of that sensual onslaught, her lips on fire where he had touched them, and he laughed again. 'I have to go,' he said. 'Back into the fray. Don't let your coffee get cold.'

She drank it in a bemused state, her mind whirling in a wonderland of overwhelming sensation. She wanted to savour the memory of that kiss for as long as she could, but after he'd left the room and reality slowly began to sink in once more, she realised that life had to go on, and she had no choice but to get back out there and join the frantic race to deliver health care to the endless queue of people who were waiting outside.

Her nerves were in a chaotic state after that unexpected, delicious kiss. Sam was beginning to get to her, and she wasn't at all sure how she was going to cope with all the frantic emotions that suddenly besieged her. Didn't she have enough to contend with right now?

She went to the sink and splashed water over her face, then

dried herself on a paper towel and ran a comb through the burnished chestnut of her hair. Feeling a little more in control of herself, she walked back into A&E and started to work her way through the list of patients still to be seen.

It was a thankless task. Noise from the waiting room erupted into the treatment rooms, and she had to battle a headache as she dealt with a succession of head and face wounds caused by various fracas, pavement falls and general wild and wanton behaviour.

She felt like shouting, 'Enough!' but of course that wouldn't do at all.

In the end, it was Sam who declared 'enough'. He looked at the ever-growing list of patients and called the nurses over to the central desk. 'We have some people who are seriously injured coming in by ambulance,' he told them, 'and they have to take priority, which means these people already here will be in for a long wait. I want to set up a nurse-based treatment centre in the annexe next door, so that you can work through those who have minor injuries and send them on their way. Michelle will be in charge. We'll divide the more senior nurses into two groups—one group to work here, the rest in the annexe. The triage nurse on duty will decide which patients go to the annexe for treatment.'

He looked around. 'Is that clear? Grab what you need from stores and take it with you, those of you who are going.'

There was shock on the faces of some of the assembled group. 'You can't do that,' one of them said. 'You're not in charge of the nurses' schedule. You can't just arbitrarily decide who goes where.'

'I've just done it,' he said. 'Take it up with your nursing manager later if you like, but right now we need you to be dealing with patients.'

'And who's going to deal with all the drunks and the aggressive patients, or even with their relatives? I'm certainly not doing it,' another nurse said.

He nodded. 'Call security if there's a problem.'

'A doctor should sign off on treatment,' yet another said. 'I'm not prepared to take responsibility if anything goes wrong. We're not covered legally.'

Sam made a short, exasperated sound. 'Yes, of course, that's true. Send all the charts to me at the end of treatment, and I'll sign them off. If there are any problems or queries, put a phone call through to Ruby or me, and if there's a patient that you think needs to be seen by a doctor, or one who rejects nurse-based treatment, refer them back here. Anybody who really doesn't want to take part should say so, but as to the rest, we need to start doing this now, otherwise we'll be over-running the waiting times, and that will put our on-going status as an A&E unit in jeopardy.'

There were murmurs of dissent, but Michelle stepped forward and started sorting out which nurses would stay and which would go to the annexe. Sam began to walk away, heading towards the ambulance bay, and Ruby hurried after him.

'That nurse was right, you know,' she said. 'You can't just decide on a whim who goes where. It isn't your place to do that.'

'And do you really think the nursing manager is going to object?' His tone was curt. 'When she comes in on Monday and understands the situation, she'll okay the measures I've taken.'

'When you've had a chance to talk her round, you mean?'

He shrugged. 'Maybe. We can't stand around debating the issue when there's a job to be done. Some patients don't need to be seen by a doctor. They turn up at A&E with sprains or cuts that can be treated by nurses. We're wasting resources if we insist that a doctor sees each one of them. Each of the senior nurses is trained to practitioner level. I don't see a problem with that.'

'The trust board might object.'

'So let them sack me.'

She glanced at him. 'You really don't care, do you?' She made a face. 'I suppose that's because you're confident they won't do that...but you could have handled the situation with a little more tact, you know, instead of upsetting the staff. You won't endear yourself to anyone by taking a do-it-or-else stance.'

'That's not a problem for me. I don't need to be universally liked. I just want to get the job done.'

She gave a sigh of frustration. 'And you'll succeed, I'm sure...but there are ways of doing it, Sam...more diplomatic ways.'

He sent her a rueful look. 'So you're standing in as my popularity gauge, are you? And it looks as though you've also set yourself up to assess the way I handle the running of the unit. Why do you want to do that? Don't you have enough to contend with already with the job and everything that's going on at home?'

'I don't want to see you at loggerheads with everyone,' she said, frowning. 'You deserve better than that. I know you're trying to do a difficult job here, but you could make life much easier on yourself if you would just manage to tone your attitude down a little. We aren't all here to jump through hoops that admin throw our way. We're here because we want to do a good job, and at the same time we want to get along with the people who work alongside us.'

'I'll bear it in mind,' he said. 'But I do think you probably have other, more important, things to worry about rather than my popularity. I'm glad you came back to work, but I still haven't worked out how you manage to do this job, with all its frustrations, and keep relatively good-natured and still cope with running things back at the farm.'

'Why wouldn't I manage it?'

'Well, for instance, you didn't take me up on my offer to send people over to help out with your crops and your animals. How on earth are you able to keep going?'

'My father is helping out by calling in every morning and evening, and Mary from next door said she'd keep an eye on things each day to make sure that everything was secure and the animals were safe. She's been great with Becky too. I suspect she likes looking after her once in a while.'

'Hmm. Well, the offer still stands for me to send people over if you change your mind.'

'Thanks.'

She worked with him over the next hour or so, helping to stabilise a teenager who had been brought in after a fall from a bridge. He had suffered several broken bones and internal injuries, along with a hairline fracture to the skull.

'We've done all we can for him for now,' Sam said, writing up the medication chart and then checking the monitors and intravenous lines. 'He needs to be transferred to Intensive Care.'

Ruby made all the arrangements and explained to the boy's parents what was happening. Then she accompanied the boy to ICU, stopping there to give details of his condition and the care he had received to Jenny, the nurse in charge.

'It sounds as though things have been hectic in A&E today,' Jenny said, 'more so, perhaps, than usual.'

'Well, we've been having some fine weather,' Ruby answered, 'possibly the best we'll get before autumn sets in. I think people are making the most of it while it lasts, so the pubs are full, and people are in high spirits in more ways than one.'

'It always happens, doesn't it? Still, maybe next week we can relax a bit. Sam's holding the fund-raiser then, isn't he?'

'That's right. I'll look forward to seeing you there, Jen.'

She took a final look at the injured boy before she left. She knew she was leaving him in good hands, but she was sad to think of how much damage the fall had done to him.

Back in A&E, the relatives of the walking wounded were becoming restless. 'Your Mr Dryden is back again,' Olivia said as Ruby glanced in at the waiting room.

'*My* Mr Dryden?' Ruby echoed. 'What makes you call him that?'

'Because I suspect he's only here because he wants to see you. He's been asking for you to treat him.'

Ruby gave a frown. 'What's wrong with him?'

Olivia glanced at the triage chart. 'A sprained wrist.'

Ruby shook her head. 'I can't deal with that right now. I need to go back to Sam to help with the people in resus. Say I'm not available and send him over to the annexe, will you?'

'I will.'

They both moved off in different directions to go on with their work, but a gang of youths spilled out of the waiting room just then, arguing with the triage nurse and pushing people out of their way. Ruby went to intervene, and Olivia said hastily, 'I'll call security.'

Ruby nodded. 'Yes, do that. Thanks.'

She went to stand in front of a young man who was staggering towards the resuscitation room, blocking his way. 'You need to go back to the waiting room,' she said.

He glowered at her. 'I'm not going back there. You can't make me. My mate needs to see a doctor. Look at him.' He draped an arm around his friend, who stared at her in a bleary-eyed fashion. 'He's bleeding from a cut on his arm, and his hand's in a right state. He's weak from all the blood he's lost, and it's messed with his head.' He lurched towards her and grabbed at the name badge she wore on her green scrubs. 'You're a doctor. You see to him.'

Ruby twisted out of his grasp and turned to look at his companion. 'Let me see your arm, please.'

The youth stuck his arm under her nose, narrowly missing her face, and then swayed with the movement, so that a waft of alcohol-drenched breath fanned her face.

She studied both the arm and the hand. His knuckles were raw from where he had been in a fist fight, and the cut on his arm was not too deep. 'The wounds aren't that bad,' she said. 'The nurse has put a temporary dressing on your arm, and you should put it back in place to keep the wound from becoming infected. Please go back into the waiting room and take a seat until a doctor's free to see you.'

'No, that ain't good enough.' His friend became belligerent and lunged towards her, pushing her with enough force so that she spun round and fell back against a wall, hitting her arm on the corner of a desk. 'You see to him now.'

'That's enough.' Sam's voice cut through the air like a whip. 'We don't have to put up with disrespect. You're out of here.' Sam strode purposefully from the resuscitation room and grabbed the youth by the collar. With one hand at the nape of the young man's neck and another tugging his flailing arm behind his back, he marched him out of the unit and into the hands of the security team who were at that moment heading along the corridor towards A&E.

Sam returned a minute or so later and propelled the injured drunk back into the waiting room and sat him down on a chair. A security officer came to stand guard by the door, preventing any more unauthorised access into the main treatment area.

Sam came to find Ruby, who was rubbing her arm and heading towards resus. 'Come into the treatment room,' he said, his voice brisk. 'You're white as a sheet.'

'I'm all right. It's a headache, that's all…too much noise, too little sleep. I'll be fine, and we have patients to see.'

'They're being looked after,' he told her. 'You don't need to worry about them right now. Besides, you should have gone off duty half an hour ago.'

'Should I?' She allowed him to usher her into an empty treatment room and submitted to being gently pushed down onto a chair.

'Let me take a look at your arm,' he said.

She shook her head. 'I told you, it's fine. I'm fine. It's just my head that hurts.'

He nodded. 'Okay, we can fix that. I'll get you some paracetamol tablets. Sit there and don't move while I go and fetch them.'

Now that she was sitting, she found she had no inclination to go anywhere, so she did as she was told and stayed where she was. When he came back a few minutes later and handed her a glass of water, along with the tablets, she meekly accepted them and swallowed them down.

'You were terrific back there,' she told him, giving him back the glass and rubbing her hands over her aching temples. 'Where did you learn to handle people like that? Do you have a secret life as a security guard?'

He gave a wry smile. 'I learned how to handle bullies at boarding school,' he said. 'The older ones would pick on the new recruits. It was bad enough when they tried their tactics on me, but when they started on my younger brother, I had to let them know once and for all who they were dealing with. They didn't try it again after that.'

She looked at him curiously. 'I guess you must have been very fond of your brother. You were both a long way from home and family, so I expect you turned to one another for comfort and companionship.'

'Yes, we did.' He made a bleak kind of smile. 'I'd always looked out for him from when we were very young, and it was a natural thing for me to do the same at school. Of course that was a long time ago. We've both moved on since then.'

'But you're still fond of one another?'

He nodded. 'It goes without saying. Why do you ask?'

'I was just wondering how much contact you have with him, now that he's up in Scotland and you're down here.'

He gave a light shrug, leaning back against the wall and watching her from a short distance. 'Like I said, we've both moved on. It's unfortunate that we're at other ends of the country, but it can't be helped, I suppose. We talk to each other on the phone now and again, and of course there's always email…but we're both busy people working in professions that are deeply involving and time-consuming.'

'So you don't get to see much of your nephews?'

He shook his head. 'Birthdays, maybe, and Christmas. I doubt they even think of me very much. They have their own lives to lead.'

'I think it's very sad,' she said, getting to her feet and studying him as he began to move towards her.

'Are you sure you're feeling up to walking about?' He studied her, his brows drawing together. 'Shouldn't you sit for a little longer? You're still very pale.'

'I need to curl up in bed and have a long, uninterrupted sleep,' she said. 'Perhaps Mum will keep Becky overnight, and I'll be able to do that.' She gave him a faint smile. 'Thank you for taking care of me. I wish I could do the same for you.'

He looked at her in astonishment, giving a small chuckle. 'Take care of me? What can you possibly mean by that?'

She gave him a sad smile. 'Perhaps tiredness is giving me a different perspective on life.' Even through her weariness, she had picked up on the faintly wistful note in his voice when he spoke about his brother and his family. He might declare that he was content with his life the way it was, but deep inside him wasn't there a yearning to be part of an open-hearted, bustling family unit? So far it had eluded him, and maybe that was why he kept his emotions in check. Perhaps it was the reason why he wouldn't allow himself to love and be loved, for fear of losing control, or even of being hurt.

She studied him thoughtfully. 'It seems to me that you're a wonderful, caring, intelligent individual, with everything going for you, but I can't help feeling that you're missing out on something very precious. I wish I could help you to find it.'

His expression was totally bewildered. 'I don't have a clue what you're talking about. What do you mean, Ruby? What are you trying to say?'

'I mean that there's more to life than work, and that doesn't seem to have occurred to either you or your brother. Don't you think you ought to try to get together with him and his family more often…perhaps even invite them over for the fundraiser? Scotland isn't all that far away, is it? Family is important, and I don't think you should let these ties wither if it's at all possible to save them.' She pressed her lips together in a faintly downward curve. 'I know it's not my place to interfere, but who knows…your brother may be wishing you'd get in touch.'

He frowned. 'Men don't look at life that way. They don't go in for all this sensitivity and sentiment type of nonsense.'

She laughed. 'No, you're probably right. That's why there are women in the world—women who know how to steer men in the right direction and smooth off all the rough edges…let their softness act as a foil for men of steel.'

He began to smile and moved towards her. 'I can go along with that.' He reached for her, letting his palms flatten on her waist as he gently tugged her towards him. 'I'd appreciate the feel of your soft, feminine curves against my body any day.'

His head lowered, and he kissed her tenderly, his lips brushing hers and slowly exploring the ripe fullness of her mouth as though he would savour its sweetness for as long as it was possible.

Ruby's lips clung to his, ripples of excitement flowing through her, filling her body with exquisite longing. Her fingers tangled with the fine linen of his shirt, and she felt the heat coming from him as though she was firing up a furnace.

After a moment or two, though, he carefully started to ease her away from him. She looked up into his eyes and tried to fathom what was going on in those blue-grey depths.

'People,' he said, as though reading her thoughts. 'Nurses, doctors, patients. They're all out there, coming and going, waiting for instructions, waiting to be seen. I should go and attend to them.' He ran his fingers through the silky fall of her hair, easing it back from her face. 'You, on the other hand, should go home. Get some rest, and then maybe you'll begin to see the world in a different light.'

She frowned. Of course he was right. She wasn't thinking straight. This whole day had been odd, from start to finish, and that could only be because she'd had a bad night and was suffering the consequences.

'I'll go,' she said, 'or I'll be fit for nothing. I have a full day ahead of me tomorrow on the farm, tending to the animals, and looking after Becky. I do wish my sister would come home. That, at least, would be one less worry. I just can't concentrate properly for wondering where she is, or whether her health is deteriorating. I keep imagining her lying ill somewhere, dazed and confused.'

'Maybe you should send her a text message to say that Becky is missing her. Tell her how her baby cries for her and won't be consoled without her mother. She might gain enough strength to be able to overcome her difficulties if she believes her child needs her.'

She was surprised that he'd made the suggestion, but at least it was a step in the right direction. He was acknowledging that Becky needed her mother and taking into account the fact that Sophie would want to come home.

She thought about it as she drove along the country lanes some half an hour later, heading back to the smallholding. What would Sophie's reaction be? Would she contemplate coming back and suffer the questions that would undoubtedly follow, or would she shrink back even further into her shell, weighed down by doubt and sickness?

She parked the car on the drive and spent a minute or two

gathering up her belongings. Then she stepped out onto the smooth tarmac, pausing to lock up. Behind her, she thought she saw a flicker of movement, but when she turned to check it out, there was only a bird flying to roost in a nearby tree.

Deep in thought, she walked towards the front porch, glancing at the honeysuckle that trailed in profusion around the door. The pale cream flowers gave off a sweet, light fragrance that filled the air, and she breathed it in, enjoying that moment of sensory bliss.

Then she heard the sound of twigs cracking underfoot, and she looked around to see who was there. 'Sophie, is that you?' Hope burned briefly inside her, but there was nothing, no sign of anyone on the drive, or even around the sides of the house. She went to look. All she could see was a grey shadow flitting against the background of the shrubbery, and she felt a shiver of alarm pass through her as another, more worrying thought occurred to her. Was she being followed? But then she guessed it must have been a rabbit scurrying to its burrow, or even a squirrel heading for one of the tall trees.

Perhaps she was even more tired than she thought and her mind was playing tricks on her. Going inside the house, she dropped her bags onto the table in the kitchen and went to phone her mother.

'Go and get some rest,' her mother said. 'Becky's fine. She's playing happily, and in a little while she'll be ready to sleep. We'll bring her over to you tomorrow around mid-morning.'

'Thanks, Mum.'

They chatted for a little while longer, and then Ruby went to soak in the bath, easing away the cares of the day. She fell into bed an hour later and slept deeply, waking in the morning as the sun filtered through the bedroom curtains.

Her parents dropped Becky off as promised, and they all had a late breakfast together before her mother and father set off on a journey to the coast and a visit to her grandparents.

'Why don't you come with us?' her father suggested, but she shook her head.

'I'll stay here in case Sophie comes back. Besides, I have work in the morning, and Craig's coming over today to see the new chicks that have hatched.'

'Oh, they're so gorgeous,' her mother said, her face breaking into a smile. Her hair was a chestnut colour, similar to Ruby's, though it was cut in a short, wavy style, and it was threaded through with streaks of grey. 'They're such beautiful little bundles of brown fluff…it was so good of Craig to bring the incubator over and help you to hatch them.'

'And good of him to show me how to care for them now that they're free of their shells.'

Ruby went to see them off, showing Becky how to wave goodbye, and then they went back into the house, and she set the baby down on the rug to play with a selection of toys.

Craig arrived a few minutes later, bringing with him a bag of ready-mixed chick food. 'They call it chick-crumbs,' he told her, 'and they'll feed on this for around a month. All they need apart from this is clean water.'

She lifted Becky up in her arms, and they went outside to the shed where the chicks were being cared for in a specially prepared brooder. Heat was provided by means of a lamp, and the chicks moved around within the area of the brooder, pecking at bits of food on the floor or falling over one another in a scrabble to reach the food trays.

'Ba-ba…ba-ba…' Becky said, her eyes widening with excitement, her body straining towards the brooder, and her hands reaching out as if she would grasp the baby birds.

'No, poppet. You can't hold them,' Ruby gently told her, holding on to her tightly. 'They're too little. But we'll stand here and look at them for a while.' She glanced at Craig, who had filled up the feed trays with chick-crumb and was now carefully removing a chick who had decided to clamber inside one of them. 'How do you think they're doing?' she asked.

'They look fine to me,' he said. 'Generally, if they're content, they will sit together and make a purring sound. If they're too hot, they'll move away from the source of heat and begin to gasp, and if they're cold, they'll huddle together and make cheeping noises. These seem perfectly happy to me.'

'Good, I'm glad.'

They moved away, going back towards the house, and Ruby said, 'I wish Sophie could see them. She used to love coming over here to see the chicks when our grandparents told us they'd hatched.'

'There's still been no news?'

She shook her head. 'I wondered if she might be hiding out around here, or at least be close by. Yesterday, when I came home, I had the strongest feeling that someone was following me, or watching me, but even though I looked around, I didn't find anyone. I sent her a text message to say that Becky was missing her, but she didn't answer. I know she wouldn't stay away unless there was a problem. I just don't know how to bring her back.'

'Could anyone else have been following you?'

'I don't know. I don't think so, but it was scary for a while. I'm not usually prone to wild imaginings, but, then again, I was tired.'

'Well, it's true the mind can play tricks on you when you've been overdoing things, and you have had a lot on your plate, lately.'

They went back inside the house, and Ruby settled Becky back down on the rug in the living room. The doorbell rang, and she left Craig to watch her while she went to answer it.

'Sam,' she said. 'It's good to see you. Come in. Is everything all right? There isn't a problem at work, is there?'

He smiled and shook his head, following her along the

hallway towards the living room. 'I just wanted to make sure that you were all right and to check that your central heating problem had been fixed to your satisfaction. My maintenance man said he had fitted a new pump for you, but you'd need to give it a trial over a few days to make sure it was working as you wanted.'

'It's fine,' she told him. 'There are no problems at all, and he fixed the slates and the roofing felt for me, so everything's drying out now. I was really pleased with what he did.'

'That's good. I was sure he'd sort everything for you. I thought maybe we could go over the arrangements for the fund-raiser if you're not too busy?'

'Yes, of course. That's a good idea.' She showed him into the living room, where Craig was down on his knees playing peek-a-boo with Becky. The baby was holding a soft book in her hands, lifting it to cover her face, and every time Craig gently tugged it down and peered over the top of it, she burst into giggles that made her whole body shake.

Craig looked up as Ruby walked into the room and came to his feet, greeting Sam with a nod and a smile.

'I wondered if Craig might come along and judge the dog show for us,' Ruby said, glancing at Sam. 'We need someone who knows what to look for, don't we?'

'That's true.' Sam's expression didn't show what he thought of that idea, but Craig seemed happy enough to go along with it.

'I don't have to work next weekend, so it shouldn't be a problem,' he murmured. 'I told Ruby that I'd been out to your estate a couple of times to tend to the horses.' He studied Sam thoughtfully. 'I don't think you were there at the time, but the stable manager was around to deal with everything. You certainly have a beautiful place. It seems to me it will be ideal for a fund-raising effort like the one you have in mind.'

'I hope it will work out all right.' Sam made a brief smile.

'All we need is good weather, although we can hold the major part of the activities in the various barns and outbuildings if there's a problem.'

Becky began to shuffle along the floor, alternately rolling, sitting and scrabbling her way towards the two men. Ruby watched her, guessing that she was intent on finding Craig, but all the baby could see from her vantage point were two pairs of trouser-clad legs.

The infant began to tug at the nearest pair, clutching the fabric with her fists and pulling herself upright onto wobbly legs. Sam looked down to see what was going on, and Becky looked up, expecting to see a familiar face.

When she saw that it was Sam whose legs she was clutching, she sank down onto her bottom and began to wail. Sam's face was a picture, a comical mix of consternation and astonishment.

'Oh, dear,' Ruby said with a laugh. 'That didn't quite work out the way she expected, did it?' She sent Sam a quick look. 'It's just that she's more used to Craig being around. He was often here when Sophie or I came to visit our grandparents, so she's grown up knowing him.'

She picked up the child and gently tried to soothe her tears, all to no avail because now that Becky was nearer to Sam, it seemed to make the situation worse, and her crying became louder.

Sam winced, and Craig made a rueful face. 'That's my cue to head for the door, I think,' he said. 'All the animals seem to be going along fairly well, Ruby, so you shouldn't have any worries on that score. I'll call in again in a few days' time to see how you're doing and find out if there's any news about Sophie. I just wish there was something I could do to help out. She's such a sweet girl, it doesn't seem right that she would have gone unless there was a strong reason. I hate to think that she's ill and needing someone to look after her.'

'I'm pinning my hopes on her answering my message,'

Ruby said, lightly jogging Becky in her arms to distract her attention. 'Like you say, she could be ill or troubled, or both.'

Craig slid his arms around her and held her close for a second or two, taking a moment to tickle Becky under her chin. 'If you have any more worries that someone might be following you,' he told Ruby, 'let me know. It will only take a phone call, and I'll come and find you.'

'Thanks, Craig. I'll remember that.'

She showed him out, waiting as he went to his car, and then she watched him drive away.

Becky had stopped crying by now, and Ruby took her back into the living room, placing her down inside the playpen, where the infant practised pulling herself up and down with the aid of the wooden bars.

'What was that about you being followed?' Sam asked, his dark brows drawing together. 'Has someone been bothering you?'

She shook her head. 'I had the feeling that someone was hanging around outside, but it was most likely just my imagination working overtime.'

'Why didn't you tell me?'

'Why would I? Anyway, you weren't here, and it happened after I left work. It was nothing.'

He looked at her oddly, and she wondered if perhaps finding Craig here had unsettled him. It couldn't have helped, either, that Becky had cried on seeing him. It was a bit like a rejection…not anything that mattered, but one more thing that put him at odds with the world.

She made a pot of coffee, and they talked for a while about how things were being organised for the fund-raiser at his family estate. 'I managed to get a local band of musicians to come along on the day,' Sam said, 'and there's a dance group who'll perform some lively, modern routines, so that should help to draw a crowd.'

'Sounds good.' Ruby glanced over at the playpen and saw that Becky was rubbing her eyes. 'I asked around and found some people who will provide refreshments. I think it should turn out to be a real success. We've sold a lot of tickets in advance, and even though we aren't asking much of an entrance fee, it looks as though that will bring in a sizeable sum on its own.'

'I just hope we'll make enough in the end to provide a boost to the A&E unit. I'm really keen to get the board to think again about closing us down, and this might buy us time, at least.'

She nodded. 'There's only one thing bothering me about all this, and it's more of a personal thing,' she said. 'I'd like it if I could bring Becky along with me. I don't want to ask Mary to watch her for such a length of time, and I know my parents would help out, but they were planning on going over to a nearby town where Sophie used to work, on the off chance she's gone somewhere familiar. They just want to look around and see if they can find anyone who's seen her.'

'That's not a problem,' Sam said. 'I thought you would want to bring her. I'll come and pick you up if you like. That way you won't have to worry about anything, and you could even have something stronger than lemonade to drink if you felt like it.'

She smiled. 'Thanks, that would be great. I'm relieved to be able to bring her along with me. Mary said she would look out for any sign of Sophie coming back to the smallholding, so all in all we have most of the options covered.' She sent him a quick, thoughtful glance. 'Did you think any more about meeting up with your brother?' she asked. 'Only, it occurred to me that he might enjoy seeing all that was going on at the family estate next weekend. It's part of his heritage, isn't it, and his boys probably don't have much idea of their true background, living where they do.'

'You don't need to concern yourself with my family or our

well-being,' he said. His features stiffened a little, as though he was disturbed by her comments. 'My background, my upbringing, my home life, isn't anything that you need to worry about.'

She looked at him, feeling chastened. Had she gone too far? He was a man of mercurial moods, one time holding her close and showing her how much he cared for her, and in almost the next breath he was mentally pushing her away.

She didn't know what to make of him, yet suddenly it dawned on her that she wanted to bridge that gap between them. She yearned to be closer to him, both in a physical and in an emotional sense, but the chances of that happening were in a state of flux. Over these last few months he had somehow managed to work his way into her heart, and she had no idea what she was dealing with.

CHAPTER EIGHT

'I DIDN'T realise how much stuff I would have to bring along with me,' Ruby said as Sam helped her with Becky's push-chair and several bags that went along with it. The day of the fund-raiser had dawned, a bright, warm, beautiful day, where the sky was a perfect, cloudless blue, and the air smelled fresh and sweet. He'd picked her up, as promised, in his gleaming silver saloon car that promised luxury and comfort and delivered it magnificently. Now they had arrived at his family's country home, and after a quick, eye-opening glance at the glorious Georgian mansion, Ruby concentrated her attention on unloading everything from the car.

'It's just that I need to have Becky's food and drink, nappies and so on with me, along with a change of clothes in case of calamities—well, you know how messy she can be with food, don't you?' Ruby added. 'And that's without the toys and odds and ends to keep her occupied throughout the day.'

'It looks as though you've come to stay for a week,' Sam murmured, his mouth curving in a smile. 'Not that I'd mind at all if you wanted to do that. I do tend to rattle about the place. Having you around to keep me company would be a more than welcome intrusion.'

She made a rueful face, trying not to acknowledge the playful gleam in his eyes. 'I doubt you'll say the same once the crowds arrive here,' she said. 'You'll probably find you've had enough of visitors for a long time. And half an hour of Becky's crying would probably be enough to put you off for ever.'

'Oh, I don't know about that.' He turned to glance at the baby, who was still strapped into her car seat, a relaxed, faraway look in her eyes, as though she was biding her time contentedly until something more exciting happened. 'I'm sure she and I will learn to get along.' He picked up the floppy bunny and moved its arms and legs in a funny dance, so that Becky giggled and reached for it, opening and closing her fists in a familiar gesture. He made it dance again, and this time she chuckled so hard that her whole body shook.

Ruby laughed. 'You've found her soft spot. She takes bunny to bed with her. She won't be parted from him, unless it's for food.'

Sam helped her to set up the pushchair and slid the bags into the rack underneath. 'I'll take you into the house and introduce you to my housekeeper, Sarah. She'll see to anything you need today and help you out with Becky if necessary.'

'Does Sarah work every day, even at the weekends?' Ruby was curious about everything to do with Sam's home life. He said very little about it, and she tried to glean bits and pieces wherever she could.

'No, we have two housekeepers who both work part-time, and generally they sort the hours between them. Sarah volunteered to come in today. Her husband and children are coming to enjoy the day out, so she can give them lunch here and generally join in the fun. She's been with us for a long time, so she's really like one of the family herself.'

Ruby unclipped Becky's restraining straps and settled her in the pushchair, leaving Sam to lock up the car. She glanced towards the house. 'It's really quite beautiful,' she murmured, 'with all that lovely stonework and those long, arched windows. When you said it was symmetrical, I was expecting something refined and austere, but it's absolutely wonderful. It's big, but it's not imposing at all, just perfectly designed with those L-shaped side extensions. And as to the grounds, well, from the front it looks like something from a landscape painting with all those mature trees as a backdrop.'

'I'm glad you like it,' he said. 'It's all been designed to be pleasing on the eye. In fact, it's more like two U-shapes back-to-back with extensions to the sides. That gives us more privacy in the gardens that are planted in the shelter of the L-shapes. You'll see, when I give you a quick tour, that we have glass doors opening out into those gardens. Around the back of the house, the outbuildings are arranged around a courtyard, with the stables to one side and the barns and grooms' quarters on the others.'

They walked towards the front entrance, where stone urns provided splashes of colour, filled with bright, flowering begonias and waxy green foliage that spilled out over the sides. The walls of the house were covered in an attractive reddish-bronze-coloured ivy that had been neatly trimmed.

'So will people be intruding on your courtyard space today?' she asked. 'I thought when you said we would be using fields for the event, everything would be staged well away from the house.'

'It will. We decided to erect some marquees on the fields, instead of using the barns. I just thought I'd show you the house and garden first, so you'll have a chance to look around. Besides, I expect you want to give Becky time to be free of the pushchair and stretch her limbs before we go and see how things are set out.'

'That would be good. That was thoughtful of you.'

Inside the house, they walked through a wide hallway and then turned into a huge T-shaped area that made up the kitchen, dining and utility room. The kitchen was magnificent, with oak beams, gleaming units and copper pans on display.

A woman Sam introduced as Sarah was bustling busily about, laying a large oak table with plates of triangular sandwiches, pizza slices, a large ham and bowls of salad. She added a selection of cheeses and fruit.

'It's good to meet you,' Sarah greeted Ruby. She was a middle-aged woman, with soft brown hair and friendly grey eyes. 'And is this young Becky that I've been hearing so much about? Would it be all right if I hold her for a while? Will she take to me, do you think?'

'Of course you can hold her. I think she'll be okay with that.' Ruby glanced at Sam. 'She does have moments when she decides to be awkward, but she seems to be in a good mood today.'

Sam winced. 'I'm on my best behaviour so as to try and make friends with her,' he told Sarah. 'I haven't had much luck with her until today.'

'Are you talking about young Becky or Ruby?' Sarah chuckled, giving Ruby a quick smile as she reached out to hold the infant. 'He told me how you speak your mind and tell him where he's going wrong. Keep on doing that, is what I say.'

Ruby felt her cheeks fill with a rush of warm colour. 'It's a habit I ought to curb,' she said. 'He is my boss, after all.'

'He still needs to listen sometimes,' Sarah murmured. She cuddled Becky. 'It never does any harm to take a moment every now and again.' She tickled the baby, making her smile, and the infant grasped the decorative buttons on Sarah's blouse, delicately testing out the size and texture of each one with her fingertips.

Watching them gave Ruby a poignant reminder of how it had been when Sophie was at home and she would lift Becky in her arms and cuddle her. A feeling of overwhelming sadness washed over her. Where was her sister? Why couldn't she find her and take care of her?

'If you two women are going to talk about me as if I'm not

here, I'm going to take Ruby away from here and show her around,' Sam said. 'Divide and conquer, that's the way I see it.'

Ruby pulled herself together. Sophie would have loved to be here. Maybe one day soon she would return, and all the heartache would be a distant memory.

Sarah laughed. 'You go ahead,' she said, looking at Ruby. 'I think Becky will be all right with me if you want to leave her for a while. I hunted out the old playpen from the attic and put it in the dining room, so she can amuse herself in there if need be.'

'That sounds perfect.'

'I forgot to tell you that Sarah loves babies,' Sam put in, his mouth tilting at the corners.

Ruby smiled. 'I can see that. That's great, Sarah, thank you.' She could see that Becky was content to be with Sarah, and if there should be a problem, she wasn't going to be far away, was she?

'And any time you want to eat, come and help yourselves to what's on the table,' Sarah suggested. 'I'll keep everything covered up so that you can pick at it as you like throughout the day, and there are plenty of cold drinks in the fridge.'

'That sounds like my kind of heaven,' Ruby said with a grin. 'Thanks, Sarah.'

She went with Sam to explore the rest of the house. The sitting room was across the hall in another T-shaped section that included a study-cum-library. 'This is where I tend to work in the evening,' Sam said, showing her into the study. 'I have all the reference books I could want in here, along with a computer and Internet connection, and I find it quite peaceful, especially after a tough day in A&E.'

'I can see how you would feel that way,' Ruby said. 'Everything is so perfect…all those bookcases, and that beautiful old oak desk…but it's comfortable in here as well, isn't it? I love the armchairs and that grand fireplace…and the view from the window…' She looked out through the wide, arched and glazed doorway to a paved terrace, and beyond that to a sweeping lawn surrounded by flower borders filled with banks of hollyhocks, asters and sweet williams in varying shades of pink through to blue. 'I could just imagine myself sitting here writing my magazine columns and keeping my medical website up to date.'

She put a hand to her mouth fleetingly as it dawned on her that he might misconstrue that, but he said softly, 'I can imagine that, too, though I tend to think of you working away on your computer at the farm, surrounded by the clutter of family life, and looking out every now and again at the pond and the meadow at the back of the house.'

'As opposed to the neat and tidy, wonderfully organized way of things here?' She gave him a wry smile. 'I have to move all sorts of bits and pieces off the desk or table before I can get down to work, and when I look outside I see a meadow full of buttercups and celandines, not to mention the odd daisy or two…and sometimes a few hens wandering about, or the ducklings following their mother to the pond. My life is very haphazard, but this all fits you to perfection.'

'Oh, I don't know…there's a lot to be said for the laid-back, relaxed and hassle-free approach. I haven't ever tried it, but I must say it has a certain appeal.'

She stared at him in astonishment. 'Good heavens, the shell is cracking, the barriers are breaking down. Wonders will never cease. Are you sure you're feeling all right? Next thing, you'll be giving it all up to go trekking in the mountains or on safari in Africa.'

His mouth curved in amusement. 'Let's not get too far ahead of ourselves. It would at least have to be gold panning in Australia.' He laid an arm lightly around her waist and led her to the door. 'I think we should continue with the tour, don't you?'

The intimacy of that gesture was enough to cause a wave

of heat to ripple throughout her body, but she tried not to think too much about that. He was intent on showing her around, nothing more, and she had to remind herself that her priority today was to take care of Becky. She couldn't simply abandon herself to thoughts of getting close to Sam, could she?

The sitting room was a haven of peace, a long, wide area, furnished with deep, luxuriously upholstered sofas, low coffee tables and graceful plant stands that held exquisite flower arrangements or trailed silvery-green fronds. The floor was pale oak, and the room was filled with light from long, arched windows and doors that opened out on to a paved area surrounded by a low stone balustrade.

The garden here was landscaped, with borders of flowering shrubs laid out in circular swathes, and rustic arches and fences here and there, covered by rambling roses. To one side, there was a carved wooden seat beneath a trellised arbour near to a rockery area with a waterfall that flowed gently into a large lily-clad pond.

'It all takes my breath away,' Ruby said softly, gazing out. 'You must be so content to live here amongst all this splendour.' She turned to face him but caught sight of his briefly bleak expression before he pulled his features into the semblance of a smile.

'I might have been,' he murmured, 'but life has ways of intruding and causing havoc.'

She gazed at him, expecting him to go on, but instead he seemed to straighten up and said quietly, 'Perhaps we should finish the rest of the tour later. I have to go and welcome everybody to the event, so, if you like, we could go and prise Becky from Sarah's arms and take her to see what's going on, or you could stay and help yourself to something to eat and drink.'

'I'll come with you,' she said quickly. 'I don't want to miss out on anything.' She didn't know what he had meant by that remark about life intruding and causing havoc, but perhaps it had something to do with his family and the fact that this beautiful house was empty most of the time, except for himself, and the people who were employed to keep the estate in perfect order.

Becky was happy enough to be settled in her pushchair once more and seemed to be very taken with the crowds that had gathered on the field to one side of the estate. Music floated over the air, a bright, cheerful tune that put everyone in the right sort of mood from the beginning. The smell of hot roast meats wafted towards Ruby as she passed by the barbecue stand, and the refreshments tent was doing a roaring trade already.

They stopped to look at the various stands, where vendors were selling all kinds of wares from autumn bulbs to necklaces and children's toys. Sam bought a colourful plastic windmill for Becky, handing it to her so that she could watch it spin in the faint breeze.

Ruby rescued it as Becky reached out to grasp the rounded tips and stopped it spinning. 'I think I'll fix it to the side of the pushchair so that you can just watch it going round,' she told her. 'We don't want the toy broken before we even manage to get it home, do we?'

Becky frowned, but once Ruby had put the windmill in place, she settled down to watch in fascination as the wind caught the plastic fronds and whirled them around, so that the colours formed a rainbow pattern.

'That will keep her occupied for a while,' Ruby said.

Sam nodded. 'Since we've reached the bandstand, I'd better go up there and do my bit,' he said. 'I'll announce the raffle and tell people about the events that will be going on, just in case they've lost their programmes.'

'And tell them what it's in aid of,' Ruby reminded him. 'Tell them to dig deep into their pockets and purses because we want to fund state-of-the-art equipment specifically for our

A&E. They can't close us down if we're the best port of call in the area, can they?'

'Will do,' he said.

He made his short speech, bringing chuckles from the crowd as he outlined the pitfalls of spending too long in the refreshments tent, or the hazards involved in shepherding children by every ice cream van on site. 'Don't get me wrong,' he said. 'I'd love it if you do that…but then again, I'm not the one driving home with youngsters full of fizzy pop and ice cream in the back of the car. Have fun,' he told them, 'enjoy the shows and please give generously. Your A&E needs you.'

He stepped down from the bandstand and showed her where there was an exhibition of country crafts. 'Your ladies from the village institute have done us proud,' he told Ruby. 'I took a peek earlier at some of the items on display. There are some lovely stained glass vases and bowls for sale. I noticed you have one or two on shelves at the farmhouse— and I guessed you like them because you have one on your desk there too.'

She nodded. 'I do have a bit of a thing for them—I'd like someday to have a collection of glass in the bathroom—high up on a beautiful bamboo shelving unit where Becky can't get hold of them.'

They wandered around the crafts tent for a while, and Ruby made a few purchases, adding a lovely bead bag to her selection. 'It's so pretty,' she said. 'It's for if and when I ever get to go anywhere glamorous and fashionable…unlikely, I know, but I can dream, can't I?'

Sam laughed. 'It may not be a dream,' he said. 'Who knows? Maybe I'll whisk you away somewhere.'

'Oh, yes? The hospital restaurant is the most glamorous place I'll ever get to, on past experience.' She said it with a glimmer of humour in her eyes, and he purposefully moved her on to the compound where the dog show was being held.

'You know you can rely on me to show you a good time,' he said. 'Dogs and puppies…what more could you want?'

She chuckled and went to find a clear place on the grass where she could release Becky from the restriction of the pushchair for a while. She lifted the baby out and set her down on a small blanket, placing her favourite toys beside her.

'Doh, doh, doh…' Becky said, stretching out her arm and indicating the dogs that paraded around the enclosed ring.

'Yes, you're right…they're doggies. Clever girl.' Ruby sent her an admiring glance. 'Well done.'

'You're not trying to tell me that she said "doggy", are you?' Sam remarked, sending her an amused look. 'That was no way a proper word.'

'Was too,' Ruby said with a defiant lift of her chin. 'Stop trying to burst my bubble. It was definitely "dog" that she said. I won't hear you say otherwise.'

He laughed and turned his attention to the show. Craig was there, inspecting all the competitors, a motley assortment of pedigree, mongrel and mixed breeds, all barking, tail wagging and generally having a wonderful time and basking in the attention of the assembled crowd.

'The winner of the small dog category is…Cup Cake, the west highland terrier,' Craig announced. 'He may be short, but he has a big personality.' Cup Cake jumped up in excitement and did a funny sort of pirouette, falling over his back legs, rolling over, and then wriggling to a standing position once more, tangling his lead around his owner's legs in the process and delighting everyone who looked on.

'Doh…doh…' Becky said again, holding out her arm and pointing towards the dogs as though she would gather them up.

'See,' Ruby hissed under her breath. 'Told you so.'

'Nah. It was nothing like "dog",' Sam declared.

Craig came over to them a few minutes later. 'Hi, you two.

Hi, Becky.' He smiled at Ruby. 'I thought you might like to see this new addition to the veterinary household…Becky too.'

He squatted down beside them and revealed, in the crook of his arm, a brown and white sleepy puppy, covered in downy fur.

'Oh, Craig…isn't he beautiful? Can I hold him? He's a boxer, isn't he?' Ruby was overcome with pleasure at the sight of the small animal. 'How old is he? Is it all right for him to be out here with us?'

'Yes, he's a boxer, and of course you can hold him.' Craig gently lowered the pup into her arms. 'We've been breeding boxers at the kennels next door to the veterinary surgery. He's twelve weeks old, so he's been vaccinated, and it's okay for him to be here. It'll be good for him to meet up with people and dogs.'

Becky broke into an excited babble of chatter, her eyes growing wide, her arms moving to touch the puppy.

'I'll hold you,' Sam said gently to her, 'so that you can lightly pat him…all right?' He looked at the infant as though expecting a response. 'I'll hold your arm, and together we'll touch him ever so carefully. We don't want to batter him, do we? He might not like it if you're too heavy-handed.' Again he watched the baby guardedly, and she looked back at him with a glance that said, 'Can I touch him? I want to do it now…let me do it now.'

Ruby cradled the puppy in her arms, stroking him lightly and showing Becky his beautiful colouring. Becky's fingers trailed over his silky fur.

He had a streak of white down the front of his face, a white chest, and the rest of him was a golden-brown colour…except for his socks. 'Look,' Ruby said in wonder, 'he has four perfect white socks.'

She looked at Craig. 'Oh, I'm done for now. I want him. I want to take him home with me. What have you done? I'll be a lost soul without him.'

Craig chuckled. 'And how would you cope with a puppy? You won't be at home to look after him, will you?'

'I could take him with me to work and sneak him into the treatment room. He'll be perfectly all right there, and Sam won't mind at all, will you, Sam?'

Sam's eyes widened in amusement. 'And how am I supposed to answer that? Why would you want to put me in the role of the evil one who denies the princess her dreams?'

'Oh, but he's so lovely,' she murmured, nestling her cheek against the puppy's silky head. 'I'm wrecked now that I've seen him. I can't bear to part with him.'

'She's broody,' Sam told Craig, as though that explained everything. 'You'd have thought looking after Becky would have put an end to all that, wouldn't you?'

'Who can tell with women?' Craig answered. 'I just knew she'd love to see him.'

'You see,' Sam said, looking at Ruby. 'It's all his fault. Blame it on him.'

'No. I won't. He did the right thing. He knew exactly how I would react.' She gave a soft sigh, offering Becky the chance of one more stroke of the soft fur, and then she reluctantly handed the puppy back to Craig.

Craig stood up. 'I have to go and judge the next category,' he said, 'so I'll catch up with you folks later.' He looked back at Sam. 'You have a good crowd here today. It's all going really well.'

Sam nodded. He let go of Becky's arm and allowed her to settle back on the blanket. She began to rub her eyes.

'It looks as though she's ready for a nap,' Ruby said. 'Perhaps I should take her back to the house and settle her down for a while?'

'That's okay by me.' Sam started to gather up their belongings. 'We'll have some lunch, and then I'll show you the rest of the place.'

They walked back across the field, with Becky once more in the pushchair. When they reached the house, Sam showed

her up to the bathroom where she could change the baby's
nappy and make her comfortable, ready for a sleep.

The bathroom was sparkling with glass fixtures and gold
fittings, with ample room for Ruby to tend to the baby. There
was even a chair where she could sit and rock her in her arms
when she was done.

'Will she be all right in the pushchair?' Sam asked, coming
to find her a while later. 'I could probably find her a crib of
some sort if need be.'

'She'll be fine in the pushchair. I'll settle her down in the
dining room if I may. I brought the baby monitor with me, so
I'll be able to listen out for her.'

He nodded. 'That sounds like a good idea. We'll help ourselves to something to eat in the kitchen, and then I'll show
you around the rest of the house and gardens.'

They had a leisurely lunch, enjoying the appetising food
that Sarah had laid out, and washing it down with a bottle of
light, sparkling wine. Ruby felt comfortably replete and
leaned back in her chair to gaze around her.

'I can't imagine how it must feel to come back here every
day,' she said in a musing tone. 'I suppose you can com-
pletely relax, knowing that you have all these people to see
to everything for you. I don't know how your parents can bear
to stay away.'

'They're very busy with all their international concerns,'
Sam said. 'They have a house in Switzerland, which is where
they stay most of the time, and there's a smaller house in the
Lake District near to one of their companies.'

'Are they planning on coming home any time soon?'

He nodded. 'They'll probably be coming back in a couple
of weeks. I doubt they'll stay for long, maybe three weeks
here and another three in Scotland, and then they'll be home
for Christmas and New Year. They seem to like that lifestyle.'

'Hmm.' She frowned. 'I don't think it would suit me at all.'

'No, but then you're a home-loving kind of woman, aren't you?' He stood up and came around the table, holding out a hand to her. 'Let me show you around.'

She placed her palm in his, and he helped her to her feet. They went upstairs, and as he showed her all the rooms she'd missed, he draped an arm lightly around her shoulders. 'It's mostly bedrooms up here, and bathrooms, but there are also a couple more studies, and then there are the dormer rooms in the attic space.'

'Are they more bedrooms?' What she had seen so far was opulence, calm, understated elegance and quality furnishings.

He shook his head. 'One's a games room, another's a sauna and the third one is a small gymnasium.'

'Good heavens…how the other half live.'

He laughed and went on with the tour, finally showing her into a study that overlooked the courtyard. Again, there were glazed doors opening out on to a small balcony bounded by a wrought iron balustrade.

She stepped out onto the balcony and saw horses being led out by grooms, who walked the magnificent animals across the cobbled yard, through an arched entrance and out towards the fields. 'Are they the horses that will give the rides around the field?' she asked, and Sam nodded.

'They'll go out for an hour or so, and then they'll rest while other horses take over. These are the non-thoroughbreds we lease out to a riding school, so they're well used to being ridden by novices.'

She moved back inside the room, gazing around at the glass-fronted wall cabinets and the bookshelves, all in pale-coloured wood that matched the desk and storage cupboards. Again, there were armchairs and a standard lamp, which changed the focus of the room from businesslike to leisurely and comfortable.

'I'm overwhelmed…again,' she said, looking up at Sam

with a smile. 'This has been such an experience, seeing the way you live. I'm so glad that you asked me to come here.'

He reached for her, placing his arms lightly around her waist. 'I'm glad that you came along,' he said. 'I wanted to know what you would think of it, and it's good that you like this place…but your reaction to the puppy beats everything, hands down.' He smiled, his gaze travelling over her in gleaming appreciation. 'You loved him so much, and you took him to your heart as though you would hold him there for ever. I have to say, I was intensely jealous back there.'

'You were?' Her eyes widened. Did he want her to hold him and love him and keep him in her heart for ever? She wouldn't have any difficulty at all in doing that. He had grown on her, worked his way into her heart and soul, and all she wanted was for him to love her in return. Was that possible?

Probably not…she answered the question herself. Wasn't she in danger of falling into the trap of loving him, losing her heart to him, only to have him move on as he had done in the past? This was a man who was wary of letting his feelings take control…and maybe his family background was to blame in some way for that.

Even so, temptation had the better of her, and she ran a hand lightly over his chest, loving the feel of him, wanting to draw him closer, to feel the brush of his lips on hers. Perhaps he sensed what was in her mind because he lowered his head towards her and kissed her tenderly, running his hands along the length of her spine and holding her against his long body, so that she was stunningly aware of every hard muscle and sinew.

Her body responded in delicious exultation at the way his hands caressed her. He stroked her back, the gentle curve of her hips, and trailed his fingers over her arms, leaving off to glide once more over the soft line of hip and thigh.

'I don't think you have any idea of what you do to me,' he murmured raggedly, his breath warm against her temple. 'I try to concentrate on whatever I'm doing, here, or at work, and you're always on my mind, luring me into a world I've never known before. I want you. I need you. You've bewitched me, taken over all my senses, so that I'm not in control any more.'

His words brought with them a heady rush of power so vibrant that it left her dizzy with sensation. Was it possible that she could have this effect on him? Was it true that this man, who was so in control of every aspect of his life, was laid waste by his need of her? A warm tide of desire flooded her veins. It was an intoxicating feeling to know that he wanted her this way.

His fingers shifted to slide over the soft swell of her breast, and she moved against him, longing to feel the touch of his hands over the whole length of her body. Her breathing was as ragged as his by now, her heart rate quickening, the thunderous rhythm rising to a crescendo of chaotic, frantic beats that threatened to overwhelm her.

His kisses had a passionate intensity that took her breath away, and all she could think of was that his thighs were pressuring hers with intimate, thrilling heat, and she wanted more, much more. Her arms circled his rib cage, and she revelled in the strength of his male body next to hers, wanting this moment to go on and on.

Only, a noise filtered into the air, disturbing their solitude and tugging them back into the real world once more.

'What is that?' Sam said with a frown, his eyes closing briefly in recognition that the moment had been torn from them.

Ruby's sensuous glow began to rapidly cool, and perhaps it was just as well that she had come back down to earth. He wanted her, but that didn't mean that he longed for her to be part of his life, that he would love and cherish her for ever, did it?

The sound came again, a faint murmuring, and she gazed around, mystified.

'It must be the baby monitor,' he said at last. 'Did you clip it somewhere?'

She drew in a deep breath. 'I put it on the desk when we came in here,' she murmured. 'I've nowhere to clip it to on this dress.'

The sound came again, but this time it was a 'doh, doh, doh' that they both heard. Ruby slowly eased herself away from him and went to check the video monitor.

She gave a faint smile. 'I think she must be dreaming of dogs and puppies,' she said. 'Look, her lips are moving, but her eyes are closed.'

He came to look down at the video screen. Sarah, his housekeeper, had come into the dining room and was checking the baby, soothing her with gentle words, so that Becky lapsed into a deep slumber once more.

'Yes, you're probably right.' He glanced at Ruby. They both knew that the moment of closeness between them was lost, but Ruby still had those warm embers of pleasure to boost her spirits. 'Dogs and puppies,' he echoed. 'You and Becky have both been pulled into that well of emotion that makes you want to care for everyone and everything, haven't you?'

'Does that seem strange to you?' she countered. 'It's the breath of life to me. It comes from being brought up that way,' she told him.

He shook his head. 'I don't get it,' he said. 'I don't hold with all this need for closeness and dependency…with animals or people. Why can't people just live for the moment and enjoy what's on offer, without getting sentimental about everything? Even Sarah has that gooey look in her eyes.'

She sent him a guarded look. So what had just happened between them? Was it purely a physical thing as far as he was concerned? Was there no deeper meaning to his kisses, no subtle invitation to share something special with him, no unspoken word to say that he cared for her?

She floundered for a moment or two then said hesitantly, 'We…Sophie and I…always had pets around us, and Becky will more than likely follow suit. We were shown from a very early age how to look after those who needed us.' She threw him an oblique glance. 'Didn't you and your brother have those same experiences? You must have had pets at some time…a cat maybe, or even a guinea pig or a rabbit?'

'No, we didn't.' He moved away from her, and she sensed the sudden tension that had risen up in him. What had happened to bring about the stiff manner in the way he stood or to cause the tautening of his features? Had she done or said something to cause this change in his mood? Was he disturbed because of the way they had been interrupted? 'Did your parents not like having pets around the place? I suppose they might tend to run amok, or be a bit smelly on occasion— but there's usually somewhere outside where cages could be positioned.'

'The occasion would never have arisen,' he told her. 'We weren't here for all that long. At least, I don't remember much about being here when we were young…and then I went away to boarding school for several years, so the question didn't come up.'

'I'm sorry,' she said, going over to him. Was he uncomfortable because she was reminding him of things that had been missing in his life…the feelings of love and security and all the things that went along with close family relationships? Was that what this was all about?

'I keep putting my foot in it, don't I?' she murmured. 'I didn't mean to rake up bad memories. I just wanted you to know that I care about you, and I want to understand what makes you the way you are. I hoped that you might feel closer to me in some way.' She laid her hand gently against his chest, wanting to establish that warmth of connection once more.

'You didn't rake up any bad memories,' he said, moving away from her, 'and it would be better for you if you didn't try to understand me or get closer to me. I don't have anything to offer other than what I am. I've never promised anything more, and I don't have any plans for the future other than to secure the A&E unit.' He pulled in a quick breath. 'As to the rest, like I said, boarding school was okay. We had a good education, and we were privileged to be able to experience that. It stood both my brother and me in good stead for later years.'

He glanced around the room. 'Shall we go back to the field and see what's going on out there? I have to draw the tickets for the raffle in half an hour or so, and I expect you want to spend some time talking to Craig and your friends from A&E.'

Ruby gave him a bewildered look. It hurt that he was pushing her away, in both a literal and a physical sense. It was like a rejection, and she wasn't sure whether he was rejecting her or the notion of close emotional ties.

She didn't want to show her despair. Instead, she nodded. 'Yes, of course. I said I'd pick out the winner of the treasure trail map too.'

She wished things hadn't ended on this restrained, sour note. Everything had been going so well, but now Sam had reverted to his former self, keeping his emotions locked in, and the barriers were firmly in place. The shutters were down, and it dawned on her that she was right to have kept a guard on her innermost feelings. He had kissed her and drawn her close and made her feel wanted, but he would not let her into his heart, the one place where she wanted to be.

CHAPTER NINE

'I HEARD that the fund-raiser made a huge amount of money for the A&E unit,' Olivia said as her gaze skimmed the details on her patient's chart. 'That's terrific news. I expect Sam's enjoying telling the hospital board all about it this morning. They're bound to reconsider the need to close us down after that, aren't they?'

'I hope so,' Ruby answered. 'Especially when you add to that all the savings we've made by cutting down on supplies, changing the prices we pay for medicines, and bringing in-house servicing contracts on board…and that's without taking the staffing changes into consideration.'

She looked at the list of patients the triage nurse had given her. 'I'll go and look at the baby with the heart murmur,' she told Olivia. 'Perhaps you could see to the woman with the blurred vision?'

Olivia nodded. 'I've looked at her notes, and I'm thinking migraine,' she said. 'I don't believe there's any need for a CT scan, do you?'

'It doesn't appear so from what we've learned so far, but do a thorough neurological check up and make certain the history is correct. Come and find me if there's anything you're not sure about.'

'Okay, I'll do that.' Olivia glanced at Ruby. 'I heard you

had some problems when you went home after the fund-raiser. James told me your neighbour thought she had seen Sophie at the house…I thought that would be good news.'

'It would, under normal circumstances…but Mary, my neighbour, wasn't exactly sure what she had seen. She said she saw someone coming out of the house, and that could only have been Sophie, surely, since she's the only other person who has a key—apart from my parents—and there was no sign of a break-in. When we looked around later, it seemed that some of Becky's clothes had been moved from where I left them, almost as though Sophie had picked them up and not put them back in the right place. Anyway, since then there's been no sign of her.'

Olivia frowned. 'James said there was something else wrong…a man had been seen hanging around the house and farm.'

'That's right.' Ruby frowned. 'I've no idea who he was, but one of the workers from a farm some half a mile away brought over some feed for the ponies and left it in the barn. He said he disturbed a man who had been hanging about by the orchard. He didn't see him well enough to get a description, but he said he was definitely alone, and when the man saw him, he took off. I don't see how he would have been able to get into the house. None of it really makes sense.'

'It must be upsetting for you.' Olivia's gaze was sympathetic.

Ruby nodded. 'It's more worrying than upsetting. It would be good to think that Sophie was close by, but I can't help thinking that the man being there was just a fluke—maybe he planned on stealing fruit or taking some of the animals. Either way, I wish Sophie had stayed to make proper contact. It's un-nerving not knowing what's going on.'

'Perhaps she'll come back. It does sound as though she wants to do that.'

'Yes, it does.' Ruby sighed inwardly as she thought about

the events of that day. Sam had stayed around to help her search for any sign that Sophie was still around, but though he'd been concerned for her, the barrier between them had stayed in place. He had made no attempt to bring back the closeness that they'd had before.

It was a mystery to her, and it left her feeling at a low ebb. She didn't know how to find the key to unlock his heart.

She busied herself with the day's work, referring the baby to a cardiac specialist, although she suspected that the heart murmur was not of great significance. The rest of her patients were easy enough to deal with, mostly uncomplicated fractures or gashes that could be sutured without throwing up too many problems.

Sam came back from his meeting with the hospital chiefs around midday, and she glanced at him, expecting him to be in a good mood. Instead he was grim-faced, and when Ruby tried to speak to him, he was brisk and efficient.

'I can't stop and talk right now,' he said. 'There's a twelve-year-old boy being brought in by ambulance, and I need to prepare for him. He's been referred to us with suspected meningitis by the local GP.'

His words put her on immediate alert. 'What can I do to help?'

'You can ask Michelle to get the isolation room ready for him. He's being given oxygen by mask, but I'll probably need to intubate him and put him on a ventilator. The paramedics say his blood pressure is low. I probably won't do a lumbar puncture right away because there are signs that his intracranial pressure is raised. Perhaps you could take blood samples for cultures and send them off to the lab while I start the intravenous lines and administer wide-spectrum antibiotics. The GP has already given him benzylpenicillin, so that's a start.'

'Do we know what other symptoms he's showing?'

'It started with a bad headache and dislike of light. He's

very upset, apparently, confused and generally unwell. There's evidence of neck stiffness and cold hands and feet.'

'Any rash?'

'Not so far. Let's hope we're in time. We should warn the intensive care unit to expect him.'

The boy arrived just a minute or so later, and Ruby assisted as Sam and the paramedics rushed him to the isolation ward. The child was semi-conscious, able to say a few words to them, but his condition was deteriorating rapidly.

'I want my Mum,' he managed in a wretched, broken voice. He kept saying it, over and over, mumbling the words to himself.

'Of course you do,' Ruby tried to console him. 'We'll make sure they know where you are. Don't you worry about anything. Dr Boyd is looking after you, and you're in good hands. He's the best there is.'

She glanced at the lead paramedic, moving away from the trolley bed momentarily. 'Are the parents coming in?' she asked quietly, but he shook his head.

'We haven't been able to contact them,' he said in a low voice. 'Nathan was on a residential school trip, and his parents are away for the week in the Andes Mountains. Apparently he's been asking for them ever since he was taken ill a few hours ago.'

He glanced at the boy, making sure that he couldn't hear what was being said. 'The headmaster has been trying to get in touch with them, but they're not at their hotel, and either their mobile phones are switched off or they're in a bad signal area. It sounds very much as though they set off early for a day's outing. Of course, now the headmaster is feeling guilty for not contacting them sooner, but he reasoned that it would be the early hours of the morning in South America when the child first complained of feeling ill, and no one knew how serious his condition was at that time.'

She pulled a face. 'That's not a good start, is it? Thanks,

anyway, Tom, for that. Do we have anyone from the school here?'

He nodded. 'The teacher in charge of the residential group is here, and the headmaster has been liaising with them.'

'That's something, at least.'

She concentrated on collecting the blood samples, all the while trying to soothe the boy, who was becoming increasingly distressed.

Sam was working calmly and efficiently as usual, putting in intravenous lines to deliver life-saving fluids and medications, all the while checking the monitors to see how the boy was coping. Things were not looking good. The boy was having difficulty breathing, and the pressure inside his head was increasing as the meninges, the protective membranes around his brain, became more inflamed.

Sam made the decision to put a tube into the boy's throat to secure his breathing when Nathan slid into unconsciousness. 'I'm giving him corticosteroids to bring down the inflammation,' he said, 'and later we'll think about adding mannitol.'

His expression was bleak, and Ruby knew that he was desperately worried about this child. They had done all they could for him over the last hour, and now all that remained was for him to be transferred to Intensive Care. Until they found a bed for him there, Nathan would remain under observation in A&E.

'Do you want to go and get a drink?' Ruby suggested. 'You look drained of energy. Have things gone badly for you today? I know you were working here before you went off to your meeting.'

'I'm okay. Michelle's gone over to ICU, so I'll stay with the boy for as long as I can,' Sam said, 'at least until she gets back.'

'All right…but if you need a break, I can take over for you.' She studied him closely, wondering what it was that had brought the bleak expression to his face. It wasn't like him to be this way. He always fought for his patients. He never worried about the outcome, but worked with whatever hand he was dealt. Meningitis could be a devastating illness, but young Nathan still had a chance to come through this.

'Thanks. I'll be fine.' He stood by the bed, looking down at the boy, and Ruby tried to work out why he should feel such an affinity for this child above all others.

She said softly, 'I went to look in on young Jason, the boy who was injured in the car crash some time ago…do you remember? His airway was ruptured, and he had to have emergency surgery.'

'Yes, I remember.' His mouth flattened. 'I asked you why you went over to ICU to see him. I can be an arrogant know-it-all sometimes, I realise that. You don't have to rub it in.' He pulled up a chair and sat down, briefly glancing at the monitors as though to reassure himself that all was well.

'I wasn't going to do that. I was just about to say that he was discharged from the hospital with his mother a week or so back. His father's out of Intensive Care and on the mend, too. And then there was the boy who fell from the bridge…he had multiple injuries, but now he's recovering nicely. So you see, there's always hope…but you know that, don't you? I'm not even sure why I'm telling you this.'

He leaned back in his chair and studied her, a heavy sigh escaping him. 'I appreciate what you're trying to do, but I just need to be here, Ruby. You don't have to stay.'

She frowned, her brows drawing together in a fine line. 'Is this anything to do with the fact that his parents aren't able to be with him? I'm sure they would want to be here if they knew what was happening.'

'Yes, I've no doubt that's right, but in the meantime he slipped into unconsciousness, asking for them.'

'We'll be here to take care of him and see to his emotional well-being when he comes round again—if they aren't here

by then. I don't know how long it takes to fly over here from
South America.'

'At least half a day, around twelve hours or so, and that's
just the flight.'

'That's not good, is it?'

'No.' He stretched out his legs in front of him. 'Not for a
boy who's seriously ill.'

She pressed her lips together. 'Did this, or something
similar to this, happen to you at some time?'

He nodded. 'I was taken ill at the same age. All I knew was
that I felt really awful, and I knew it was something bad. I was
on my own at boarding school at that time…my brother was
only ten years old, so he hadn't joined me then, thank heaven,
or he might have gone down with the same illness.'

His mouth twisted in a grimace as he thought back over
those years. 'I remember feeling unbelievably lonely. There
was no family around, no one from home to comfort me and
tell me that I would be fine, they would take care of me…just
virtual strangers, the teachers and the boys. There was the
matron, of course, but she was an austere, no nonsense kind
of woman. "You have a sore throat, boy, and a bit of a
headache? Trying to get out of doing our maths homework,
are we?"'

'Did you have the same illness as Nathan? Was it meningitis?'

'Yes, it was. Of course, they didn't realise that at first, but then
I collapsed, and they called for an ambulance. I recall being lifted
up and placed on the trolley bed. The paramedics were wonderful, so calm, caring and friendly. I think they were my salvation,
along with the doctors and nurses who looked after me. I think
they were the real reason I turned to medicine as a career.'

He smiled. 'The paramedics even came to see me each day
as I was recovering in hospital.'

'And your parents?' Ruby was still frowning. No wonder
he felt such a bond with Nathan.

'They were half the world away. They came as soon as they were able, but I think it took several days—it was a while before the school managed to get in touch with them, and then flights had to be arranged. My grandparents were away, too, but I recall they made it to the hospital before my parents.'

'It must have been awful for you, feeling so ill and being isolated from those you loved.' Ruby went to stand beside his chair, laying a comforting hand on his shoulder.

He shrugged. 'It wasn't so bad. I was used to being away from them by then, though I did miss my little brother. When you're away from home, you learn to steel yourself against any adversity. It doesn't do to confide your feelings to anyone. That's the quickest way to be laughed at, sneered at, generally made to feel a fool, so you toughen up fast.'

'Oh, Sam, that's too hard to bear…a vulnerable child so far away from everyone who means anything to him.' She leaned over the back of his chair, nestling her cheek against his head and wrapping her arms around him. 'I just need to hug you.'

He made a soft laugh. 'I'm a grown man, Ruby. There's no need to hug me better.'

'I'm not hugging *you*. I'm hugging that lost and lonely boy.' She kissed his cheek tenderly, and then nuzzled her face against his, so that he turned in his seat and stood up, coming to hold her close.

'You're very sweet,' he said, 'and I thank you for that, but I'm okay, really. The boy inside is okay. You don't need to worry about either of us.'

He slowly released her, and she realised that someone was approaching from outside the room. Then Michelle walked in, and Ruby guessed that Sam must have heard her coming.

'ICU should have a bed for Nathan later this evening,' Michelle said, 'and the headmaster has finally managed to get a message through to his parents. They're booking the next flight back.'

'That's good,' Sam murmured. 'Let's hope he's on the mend by the time they get here.'

Michelle glanced through the instructions on the medication chart. 'That looks straightforward enough,' she said. 'You can leave him with me now, and I'll let you know if anything changes.' She gave Sam a concerned look. 'You must be devastated by the news this morning...I've just seen the chief executive officer in ICU, and he says the hospital trust is still planning to close this place down, even after all you've done. I don't understand how they can be so blinkered.'

Ruby gasped. 'That can't be true, can it?' she asked, sending Sam a shocked glance.

'That's what the chief said,' he acknowledged. 'But the hospital trust board is having a further meeting this afternoon at the Heritage, so I still have a chance to sway them.' He looked at Ruby. 'I need you to come with me to that meeting, Ruby. I know it's short notice, but you're off duty this afternoon, aren't you? Between us, I think we can persuade the executives that they will be making a mistake in closing us down. Will you do it? I'm relying on you. I need you to be there.'

'Yes, of course I'll do it, but how will I be able to help?' Ruby looked at him in consternation. Michelle had moved to the bedside to record observations on their patient and was noting down temperature, respiration and heart rate on the chart.

'You've kept a record of all the patients we've treated in the past three months, haven't you...especially those who wouldn't have made it if they'd had to be diverted to the Heritage.' Sam pulled in a deep breath. 'You'll be able to tell them about the ones you treated personally...like young Jason, for instance. He's still around because of you, and because he was brought here in good time.'

'That sounds like a great idea. I keep the file in the office. I thought it might come in handy one day.'

'Good. I'll come and find you at three o'clock, and we'll drive over there. Do you need to make arrangements for Becky?'

She nodded. 'Mary's looking after her today. I don't think she'll mind having her for a bit longer, but I'll ring up later and find out.'

They left Michelle to observe young Nathan and walked together towards the central area of A&E. 'It's no wonder that you were feeling so bad about everything,' Ruby commented. 'Having to deal with a meningitis case immediately after that meeting must have been the final straw.'

'It was just a temporary setback,' he murmured. 'I won't let these things defeat me.'

She sent him an oblique glance. 'No, that's not your way, is it? In fact, I think I've finally found the key to what makes you tick. I've been searching all this time and wondering why it is that you avoid deep, long-lasting relationships…because it isn't by chance that you've never settled down, is it? It's a choice, albeit maybe a subconscious one, that you made a long time ago. You don't let anything get to you. It's the reason you don't fall in with the social scene at work…because if you avoid people and don't get involved in meaningful relationships, nothing and no one can hurt you.'

'Pure guesswork,' he said. 'It's all nonsense.'

She shook her head. 'No, it isn't. All those years ago, when you were a child, you learned how to protect yourself from being hurt. If boys were cruel and made taunts, you showed them you didn't care. If your family was scattered over different parts of the globe, you told yourself it didn't matter. And if any woman should be foolish enough to make any impact on your emotions, you put up the barriers and send her on her way. Why would you allow anyone to get close to you, when they might wrench your heart from you and then abandon you to oblivion once more?'

He gave a short laugh. 'You have it all worked out, don't

ou? That clever, inquisitive mind of yours has been busy, and
ou've come to all the wrong conclusions.'

She smiled, turning to face him and trailing a hand lightly
ver his arm. 'No, I haven't. They're all the right conclu-
ions, and you're trying to push me away again. You want me
o think you don't care, but I have the measure of you now,
nd I'm not going to be fobbed off that easily. I know you care
bout me, maybe even love me, but you'll do your level best
o stop me from getting too close.' Her gaze meshed with his.
It's too late for those sorts of tactics, though. I'm forewarned
nd forearmed, and I'll muscle my way in no matter what
efences you try to put up.'

'You're living in a fantasy world,' he said. 'I told you a long
while ago that I don't do commitment. Why do things have
o get serious when we can simply enjoy what we have for
he moment? I tried to warn you, but it seems you didn't
isten. Don't fall for me, Ruby. I'll end up wrecking your life
ecause I can never be what you want me to be. This job is
what matters to me. It's what I've fought for, worked for all
hese years. And now, when I have to concentrate fully on
aving this unit, you're distracting me with talk of loving and
aring. It's the puppy all over again…soft, romantic, mushy.
That isn't my world.'

Ruby's eyes widened. He didn't really mean what he said,
did he? She had stung him with her insight into what made
im what he was, and he couldn't handle it. That was it,
wasn't it? Why else would he say such hurtful, cruel things?

He walked away, heading for the ambulance bay in search
of his next patient, leaving her to stand forlornly in the middle
of A&E, wondering why she couldn't pull herself together.
She was the laid-back one, the one who didn't let life get her
down, and here she was, feeling the sting of tears behind her
eyelids. Soft, romantic, mushy…was that how he saw her?
What was wrong with any of that?

'Shouldn't you be going off duty?' Olivia interrupted her wayward thoughts, and Ruby glanced at her watch.

'Oh, yes, you're right. Only, I need to make a phone call first.'

Olivia gave her a puzzled glance, but Ruby didn't stop to explain. She went over to the booth where the phone for private calls was situated and dialled Mary's number.

'How are things going?' she asked her neighbour. 'Is Becky all right…only, I wondered if you might be able to look after her for a couple of hours longer this afternoon? I have to go to a meeting.'

'Oh, Ruby…I'm so glad you called. I've been trying to get in touch with you, but the hospital switchboard has been so busy.' A note in Mary's voice alerted her to the fact that something was definitely wrong. There was a hint of panic, a nervous agitation that threatened to spill over and stop her from speaking.

'What is it, Mary? Is it Becky? Is she ill? Has she had an accident?'

'No, no…it isn't that. It's Sophie. She came back. She…she seemed fine, but then… It was… I don't know what to do…'

'Mary, please, slow down. Start at the beginning.' Ruby's heart began to hammer a tattoo. Sophie was back? But something was obviously not right. Had something happened to her? Had she taken Becky? She forced herself to stay calm. She said carefully, 'You said Sophie has come back. Is she ill or hurt in some way?'

She heard Mary pull in a shuddery breath. 'She said she had been ill. She went to see a doctor in the place where she's been staying, and he did some tests and gave her some tablets to take…a thyroid problem, she said.'

'Thyroid?' That sounded like one of the possibilities that had been running through Ruby's mind in these last few weeks. It would account for the tiredness and confusion, even for the lapses in memory, but she still couldn't see why that would cause Sophie to go away and leave her baby.

'All right, so she's back home now, and she's feeling better, is she? So what's upsetting you? Has she taken Becky somewhere?'

'No, no...it's nothing like that.' The frantic note was back in Mary's voice. 'I was so pleased to see her, but there's this man...he followed her, you see...she said he'd been following her for a long time...and now he has Sophie and Becky trapped in the house, and I called the police, but no one came, and I don't know what to do. I told them...this man, he grabbed her, and he locked all the doors and bolted them...and I can't get in to help her, and I don't know what to do.'

Ruby felt a shockwave reverberate through her whole body. 'Mary, call the police again and find out what's happening. How long ago did you phone them?'

'About an hour ago. They said, did he have a weapon, and I said, no, I didn't see one. I think they had the idea it was just a domestic incident. They say they're really busy right now...I just don't know what's happening.'

'Never mind. Phone them again. I'm coming home, Mary. I'll be with you in a few minutes.'

She cut the call and went to grab her jacket and bag from the locker room. Then, just as she was about to leave, she caught sight of Olivia on her way to a treatment room.

'Olivia...will you send a message to Sam for me? Tell him I can't manage this afternoon's meeting. Something's come up.'

'I'll do that. Is it a problem at home? You look as white as a sheet.'

Ruby nodded. 'It's something quite serious. I have to go. Tell him I'm really sorry to let him down, but something bad has happened, and I need to go home straight away.'

She hurried away, rushing out to the car park and setting her car in motion. Her mind was racing in tune with the engine. Who was this man who was holding her sister captive? Why would he be doing that?

And how would Sam react when he discovered that she would not be going to the meeting? She didn't want to let him down, but her sister's and Becky's safety meant more to her than any work-based problem. They were her family, and they needed her.

If Sam couldn't see that, then he was a lost cause.

CHAPTER TEN

'MARY, are you there?' Ruby stopped pounding on her neighbour's door and shouted through the letterbox. 'Mary, I need you to tell me what's happening.'

She heard bolts being drawn back, and finally Mary opened the door. Her neighbour was distraught, running shaking fingers through her soft brown hair. 'I'm so glad you're here,' Mary said. 'I called the police again, and they said they would send someone, but they only have a couple of policewomen available. I don't see how they're going to be able to deal with a crazy man, do you? I tried to call the farmer up at the lodge to see if he could help, but his wife said he was out on the field with the tractor. She said she'd go and find him and tell him what was going on.'

'That's something, anyway. We need all the backup we can get.' Ruby wished Sam were here. He would know how to handle the situation, wouldn't he? He wasn't one to let things faze him. But he wasn't here, he was at his meeting…that was what mattered to him most of all, he'd said so. He'd told her in no uncertain terms that she would never fit into his life on any permanent basis, and that hurt. It hurt badly.

She pulled in a deep breath. 'Did he say anything, this man who has Sophie? Did Sophie say she knew who he was?'

'She didn't say anything much at all. She'd only been here

a short time, and I could see she was desperate to see Becky
We'd been talking in the kitchen, and then she went to fetch
Becky from the back garden, where she'd been snoozing in
her pushchair. She'd just lifted her up when this man came and
grabbed her, and she held on to Becky and tried to twist away
from him, but it was impossible. He dragged them both away.
I ran out to try and stop him, but he had her in the farmhouse
before I could get to her. I think she must have gone there first,
looking for you, or Becky, and she left the door unlocked.'

She started to shake all over, and Ruby went and put her
arms around her. 'We'll get her back, Mary,' she said, with
more confidence than she felt. 'He can't mean to hurt her,
surely? Why would he want to do that?'

Ruby was beginning to wonder whether this was the man
who had been disturbed in the orchard by the farm hand just
a few days ago. Had he followed Ruby home from work
before that? Was that why she'd felt there was someone
moving through the shrubbery that day? Perhaps he had been
watching the house, waiting for Sophie.

'I need to find a way to get into the house,' she said,
thinking aloud.

'But the doors are locked and bolted,' Mary said. 'I heard
him doing it. I heard him shouting, telling her to be quiet or
he'd hurt her, and then little Becky started to cry. She must
have been so frightened, poor thing.'

'I could get in through the skylight,' Ruby said. 'If I can
get up onto the side roof extension, there's a skylight that I
can prise open. I just had the roof fixed, but the skylight still
needs repairing. The catch is faulty, and I didn't get round to
having it mended. What we need is a ladder.'

'I have a ladder,' Mary said. 'It's in the garage…but isn't
it too dangerous for you to be up on the roof…and what if he
sees you?'

'I'll just have to take my chances. The skylight is positioned quite low down near to the eaves, so I should be able to reach it fairly easily from the top of the ladder. As to him seeing me, perhaps we can distract him some way if it looks as though he might do that. If I can get into the house through the skylight, I should be able to unbolt the doors and give Sophie a means of escape. I need to take him by surprise.'

Mary was shaking her head and pressing her hands together in an agitated fashion. 'It's too risky. You don't know who you're dealing with.'

Ruby pressed her lips together. 'Correction. He doesn't know who he's dealing with.'

She went with Mary to find the ladder, but as they were carrying it from the garage, she heard a car draw up by the house. Was it the police at last?

'What on earth are you two doing?' Sam said, getting out of the car and coming towards them.

'Shouldn't you be at the meeting?' Ruby queried in surprise. She carefully manoeuvred the ladder onto the driveway and set it down.

'Forget the meeting.' He was grim-faced again, looking from her to Mary and back to the ladder. 'Tell me what's going on here. Has Becky found herself locked in the house, somehow? Why do you need a ladder?'

Ruby quickly told him what had happened. 'He has my sister, and he threatened to harm her. The police are supposed to be on their way, but it's been almost two hours now, and there's still no sign of them. I have to get in there and help Sophie.'

'And what are you planning on doing when you come face to face with him?'

'I haven't really thought that far.' She made a face. 'Threaten him with a broom handle?'

'No.' Sam looked across to the farmhouse, assessing the scale of the problem. 'You don't have to do anything of the sort. I'll tackle him.'

Ruby bit back a retort. She was ready to do whatever was necessary, but when it came down to it, Sam was bigger, stronger and altogether more of a threat to any man than she was, and she wasn't fool enough to argue with him over that. 'I'll come with you,' she said.

'I'd rather you didn't.' He turned to Mary. 'Do you have a toolbox handy? I need something I can use to lever the window up.'

Mary seemed to be less nervous now that a man had arrived. 'Would a chisel do? My husband has all kinds of tools in the garage.'

He nodded, and she went back into the garage and rummaged around on one of the shelves.

'Here you are,' she said, coming back to him.

Ruby sent him an anxious look. 'You will be careful, won't you? We don't know if he has a weapon of any kind. If you manage to unbolt the front door once you're inside the house, we can come in and help.'

He laid a hand lightly on her arm. 'I want you to stay here, out of the way, where I know you'll be safe,' he said. 'I haven't turned my back on everything that's important to me to come and make sure you're all right and then have you mess it up.'

She gazed at him. It wasn't exactly the best way of saying that he cared about her, but it was a start, and if it hadn't been for her worries about Becky and her sister, the mere fact he'd said it would have made her heart jump in exhilaration.

'Should we cause a distraction?' Mary asked, but he shook his head.

'No.' He gave them an exasperated look. 'Do nothing. Both of you stay here.'

They didn't of course. There was no way Ruby was going to stand back and let him walk into danger and not be there to help him out if need be. Nor was she about to leave her sister's welfare to other people, even if it was Sam who was taking control of the situation.

As soon as Sam disappeared with the ladder around the side of the farmhouse, they crept towards the front of the building. Once there, Ruby whispered to Mary to stay under cover, while she headed after Sam.

Without making a sound, he had the ladder against the wall, and then he climbed up, pausing at the top to reach up and lever the window open. Ruby found herself praying that the man inside the house wouldn't hear him.

When Sam disappeared into the house through the skylight, Ruby followed. She climbed up the ladder, taking care not to look down, and then eased herself into the attic room through the window.

Sam was already on his way down the stairs, and she crept silently after him, making her way into the hallway. Sam was listening for sounds of voices, and once he had located them in the living room, he set off in that direction. He hadn't unbolted the front door, so Ruby made that her first objective. She carefully slid back the bolts and quietly opened the door.

Outside, she saw that the farmer had arrived. Craig was with him, and when he saw Ruby, he started towards her. Ruby stopped him, shaking her head and putting her finger to her lips to show him that he needed to be quiet. Perhaps it wasn't a good idea to have everyone barge in just then.

Mary was speaking in a low voice to the farmer, and after a while he frowned and reached into his Land Rover for a metal bar. Craig went to speak quietly to him, and Ruby guessed they were discussing strategies.

Ruby left the door ajar and went back inside the house. She armed herself with an umbrella from the stand by the door and headed towards the dining room. She stood, half hidden by the recess of the glazed archway that led into the living room, and listened to what was going on inside the room.

'No one's going to take Sophie away from me,' the man was saying. 'She belongs with me.'

Ruby recognised Nick Dryden, her patient who she'd operated on recently.

'Put the baby down, Nick,' Sam said in a calm, authoritative voice. 'She's not a problem to anyone. You don't need to involve the baby in any of this.'

'It should have been my baby,' Nick answered, a bitter note in his voice. 'Sophie's mine. She didn't want to have this baby. She wanted to be with me. That's why she went away. She doesn't want this baby.'

Through the small opening between the door and the frame, Ruby could see Sophie's horrified expression. She was shaking her head, her hands reaching out for Becky, who was screaming relentlessly, her small face reddened and streaked with tears. Nick was holding her with one arm, his stance threatening, his features etched with rage.

'You're delusional,' Sam said in a quiet tone. 'It's what comes from taking drugs like ecstasy, benzodiazepines and amphetamines, among other things, over the last few years. You've tried all of those at one time and another, haven't you, Nick? It's written in your notes at the hospital, and that's why you're always turning up at A&E, complaining of pain and anxiety and wanting drugs to calm things down. That's why you're shaking and restless right now, and why your breathing is rapid.'

'Sophie's my woman. She loves me. I love her. I've always loved her, ever since I first saw her.'

'Perhaps she'll go on loving you if you treat the baby with love and compassion,' Sam suggested. 'Why would she love a man who would threaten her child?'

Nick appeared to think about that. Uncertainty showed in his eyes, and he looked at Sophie, who followed Sam's lead and began to nod.

'That's right,' she said. 'Won't you put Becky in her playpen so that you and I can talk? That's what you want, isn't it? We can't talk while you're holding her like that.'

Nick hesitated, and then he carefully relinquished his hold on Becky, placing her down in the playpen across the room. Sophie moved towards him, putting herself between Becky and Nick, and at the same time Sam took a slow step closer to both of them.

'This is the police.' A woman's voice cracked out along the hallway, making Ruby jump. 'Miss Martyn…Miss Sophie Martyn…are you in there? Are you all right?'

Nick Dryden, startled by the sudden intrusion, ran towards the glazed archway, looking for a means of escape. He flung open the door, and Ruby intercepted him, lifting the umbrella and pointing the sharp, elongated tip towards his midsection like a gun.

'I'd stay there if I were you,' she said succinctly, 'unless you'd like another incision near where your spleen used to be.'

Startled by her sudden appearance, and uncertain about the threat, he hesitated, and that was his undoing because Sam launched himself at him and grappled his arms behind his back. 'You're not going anywhere,' Sam said in a terse voice, 'except to the police station.'

Two policewomen came into the room and, within minutes, Nick had been handcuffed and cautioned. They led him away to the waiting police car.

Ruby, in the meantime, went over to Sophie and wrapped her arms around her. 'I'm so glad you're safe,' she said raggedly. 'I've been so worried about you.'

Mary looked around at the gathering of people. 'Perhaps I should go and make a pot of tea,' she said. 'We're all a bit shaken up, aren't we?'

The farmer nodded. He relinquished his iron bar now that all was well. 'I guess I won't be needing this now,' he said to

Craig. 'It's a good thing you were at the farm with me. Between us, we'd have made a good team.'

Craig smiled. 'You're right.'

Becky, sitting surveying all that was going on, and still uncertain about the ordeal she'd been through, decided that she wanted out of the playpen. Tearfully, she stretched out her arms so that someone, anyone, would lift her out of there, and Sam went to the rescue.

'You want your mother, don't you, young lady?' he said, picking her up and comforting her.

Ruby was still hugging Sophie, not wanting to let her go. 'Was that man the reason you went away?' she asked.

Sophie nodded. 'I was confused and afraid,' she told Ruby. 'He had been bothering me for months, ever since I ran into him at the health centre one day. He seemed to take to me for some reason, and he had the idea that I returned his feelings. I didn't even know him.'

'Why didn't you tell me what was going on?'

Sophie sat down on the sofa and held out her arms for Becky. 'I didn't really understand any of it. I was feeling so awful. I was tired all the time, a bit panicky and depressed. I thought it was post-natal depression and that I would get over it eventually.'

Sam settled Becky in the crook of Sophie's arm, and she kissed her cheek and hugged the infant close. Becky snuggled into her, little fingers clasping her mother's cotton top as though she would never let go.

Ruby sat beside her on the sofa and waited for her to go on. 'But the depression didn't go away, did it?'

'No. Things just seemed to be getting worse, and I was forgetting things all the time. I tried to go to the health centre, but he was there a lot of the time. Then, one day, he threatened me. He said if I didn't go with him, he would hurt Becky.' She swallowed, remembering the incident and struggling to keep her composure. 'I managed to get away from him, and I thought, when we go to the farmhouse, we'll be safe. He won't know where to find us. Only, he turned up again, and I knew I had to go. If I wasn't around, he wouldn't be able to get to Becky, would he? He wouldn't know where she was. It was me he wanted, and he wouldn't go after Becky if I wasn't there.'

She stroked Becky's arm and back, keeping her close. 'I couldn't stay away, though. The doctor gave me some tablets to take, and after a few weeks, I started to think clearly again. The doctor said sometimes in pregnancy the thyroid can be affected, like an autoimmune problem, where the body turns on itself, and mine wasn't producing enough of the hormones I needed. He said it could be treated, and it turned out that he was right.'

'Do you feel better now, in yourself?'

Sophie smiled. 'I'm getting there. I'm just relieved to be back and to have Becky with me once more.'

Craig came to join her on the sofa, putting an arm around Sophie's shoulders. 'I've missed you,' he said. 'I wish you had told me what you were going through. I'd have done whatever I could to help you.'

Sophie gave him a wavering smile, and he hugged her close. Ruby stood up, leaving them to talk for a while. She went to chat with the farmer and Mary, letting them know how much she appreciated their help.

'It was really good to know that you were there when I needed you,' she told them. She looked at Sam. 'You, too, Sam. You were marvellous.'

'You should have told me what was happening, back at the hospital,' he said. 'There's no way I would have let you deal with this on your own.'

The farmer drank his tea and put his cup down on the table. 'Any time you need me,' he told her, 'you only have to call.

I'm glad you decided you wanted to stay on here. It'll be
great having you as a neighbour. You always had a soft spot
for this place, didn't you?' He nodded to Mary. 'Thanks for
the tea, but I must be going. I've a field of corn waiting to be
harvested.'

'I'll see you out,' Mary said. 'Then I'm going to stay for a
while and talk to Sophie…' she glanced at Ruby '…if that's
all right with you?'

'You know you don't need to ask, Mary. Stay as long as
you like.'

Sophie and Craig were deep in conversation, with Becky
sitting contentedly on her mother's knee. Ruby turned to Sam
and said, 'Shall we walk outside for a while? I want to know
how you gave up on the meeting so easily. I would never have
expected you to do that.'

They walked down to the paddock, where the two
Shetland ponies were grazing contentedly. Ruby stopped
for a moment or two, going into the barn to find oat cakes,
and when she came out, Sam was answering a call on his
mobile phone.

'You're joking?' she heard him say. 'And what did they
make of that?' He listened. 'Good heavens. I wasn't expecting anything quite so dramatic.' He gave a short laugh and then
sobered. 'Is there any news of the boy with meningitis?' He
nodded. 'Thanks, James. You did a fantastic job.'

He cut the call, and Ruby sent him an enquiring glance.
'What was all that about?'

She handed him an oat cake, and he looked at it doubtfully,
asking, 'What am I supposed to do with this? Do I eat it?'

'Not unless you're hoping to live like a Shetland pony,' she
said in a dry tone. The ponies began to trot towards them,
tossing their heads in gentle expectation. 'You feed it to them.'

'Oh, I see.' His mouth curved. 'I was just kidding. We feed
these to the horses back at home.'

She gave a wry smile. 'So, I guess that was a call from the hospital. Is Nathan's condition still the same?'

'He's a little better, if anything. His heart and respiration rate have improved slightly, and there are signs that the corticosteroids have reduced the inflammation around his brain. It will take a while for the antibiotics to do their job, of course, but there's no sign of a rash, and in general he appears to be responding to treatment.'

She gave a long sigh. 'That's such a relief.'

'Yes, it is.'

Ruby stroked both of the ponies for a moment or two and then said, 'Shall we walk over to the summer house? I don't think you've seen that part of the farm, have you? It's at the far side of the pond, hidden from view by a pergola.'

They set off, arriving at a landscaped clearing. 'It looks like a beautiful sunny position here,' Sam said as they reached the cedar-wood building.

'That's what we thought. My grandparents chose this aspect specifically. We all like to come and sit out here sometimes…especially when the ducklings have hatched and they come waddling after their parents. They often trek from the pond to the stream across this stretch of land.'

She stepped onto the veranda of the summer house and opened up the glazed doors to reveal a cushioned hammock inside. The veranda was bordered by wooden rails, and to each side was a tub planted with trailing fuchsias and colourful surfinias.

'I love being out here,' she murmured, taking a seat on the hammock and inviting him to sit beside her. 'It's so peaceful, with just the sound of birdsong to keep me company. If I have things on my mind, I can sit here and think them through. It always helps.'

He sat down beside her. 'You're a very peaceful person, aren't you?' he said with a smile. 'It's what I like about you.

I see things in straight lines, in black and white, and you're soft pastels and undulating patterns. You manage somehow to blur the edges for me and show me where I'm going wrong.'

She let her glance trail over him. 'But you don't go wrong, do you? You have a focus, and it's what you need to keep you on track. There's nothing to say that you can't follow a line, but sometimes the line might bend a little and take you along a more leisurely path.' She hesitated. 'Like the way you handled the restructuring of the A&E unit. You knew where you wanted to be, but to get there you had to meander a little in order to bring everyone on board. You managed it in the end, even if the executives threw a spanner in the works. You set out to streamline the unit, and you achieved your objective.'

'There is one area where I went badly wrong.' He frowned, his gaze watching her subdued expression. 'I let you believe that your summary of my character was way off beam, but that wasn't true. I just didn't want to admit that you'd found my Achilles heel. That would leave me vulnerable, and you, of all people, by simply rejecting me, would have the power to reduce me to nothing. Then I realised that without you, I *am* nothing.'

He smiled, lifting his hand so that his fingers could trace the line of her cheek. 'I've never felt this way before about anyone. I said I didn't believe in commitment, and that was true enough, but only in so far as I've never met anyone I loved before this. I never had any reason to make a commitment to a woman.'

She gazed at him, her heart making a frantic little leap inside her chest. 'You love me?' she echoed.

He reached for her hand and cupped it between his palms. 'I do love you,' he murmured. 'I love everything about you, and it grieves me that I've been fighting it for so long. I knew, almost the first time I saw you, that you were unique, special,

ie one woman who could take my heart, and, if you chose
), you could wring everything from me. I didn't want to open
iyself to that kind of hurt…but in the end I've come to realise
iat life would be so much more painful without you.'

He looked into her eyes. 'I love you, Ruby. You're my
ɔulmate, everything I've ever wanted, and you alone could
iake me into a whole person once again…because up to now
've been fragmented, missing that one special ingredient that
/ould hold me together.'

She leaned towards him and kissed him full on the mouth.
I love you, Sam. I feel as though together we can move
nountains, but all I really want to do is have you and hold you
.nd share my life with you.'

He released a long, pent-up sigh. 'You don't know how
;ood it is for me to hear you say that.' He hesitated. 'Will you
narry me, Ruby?'

'Yes, Sam, I will.'

They smiled into each other's eyes for a long time, simply
iolding one another, leaning back in the hammock and feeling
:he gentle, soothing motion as it rocked to and fro.

Then Sam said quietly, 'Would it be all right with you if
we bought this house and farm together? You said you wanted
to live here, and that's what I want, too.'

'Of course we can do that. I just never thought you'd take
to somewhere as haphazard as this.'

'I love this place. It's so much like you. Natural, relaxed,
peaceful and great fun.' His mouth tilted at the corners. 'We
could even ask Craig if that puppy's for sale…the one that
stole your heart and filled me with jealousy.'

She laughed. 'Is that why you said it was romantic mush?
I was very upset about that, you know.'

He gave a shrug. 'I admit, I'm not perfect.' He had the grace
to look sheepish. 'But it occurred to me that if you wanted to
work part-time, you'd be able to take care of him…and maybe

Sophie and Becky would like to play a part in that, too, especially if they decide to live nearby.'

'That sounds like a wonderful plan…except that I probably won't have a job at all, will I? Didn't the trust board decide to close us down? You didn't go to the meeting, so I imagine it all fell through.'

He sent her a considering look. 'Actually, I think we may have won after all.'

She raised her brows at that. 'What makes you think so?'

'I asked James to step in for me at the meeting. It was a lot to ask of him, I know, because he's only an SHO, but he's turning out to be a very capable young man. I gave him your file, and I also handed him my analysis of how we'd made savings and obtained more funding.'

'So James went in and managed to sway them?'

'Not exactly. Apparently a whole load of protesters marched on the Heritage, where the meeting was taking place, and demonstrated their feelings about the threatened closure. The press were there, too, and the executives were more than a little taken aback.'

Ruby was puzzled. 'Who organised the protest? It was very sudden, wasn't it? Did it have anything to do with you?'

'Only indirectly. Partly, it was a reaction from a lot of people who came to the open day. I think some of the staff at the hospital let it be known that this morning's meeting had a negative outcome.' He leaned back in the hammock, twisting around to face her more squarely. 'The rest of it might have had something to do with my brother.'

Ruby frowned. 'I don't think I follow.'

'I took your advice the other day,' Sam explained, 'and phoned my brother to see if he wanted to come down here for the fund-raiser. He couldn't manage it, but he was really interested in what was going on. My parents have always funded the local hospitals, you see, because they were so appreciative of the way I was looked after when I was taken ill. My brother was considering setting up a trust fund himself along the same lines, and he asked me if I would think about joining him in that. I said I would, provided that the A&E unit remained safe.'

'So…let me get this straight…was your brother the one who notified the press?'

He nodded. 'I believe so. I rang Robert this morning when I came out of the meeting with the hospital chiefs and told him what had happened. He must have phoned a few friends and passed the word around. Then he talked to my parents and explained the situation to them. According to James, who was at the second meeting this afternoon, the trust board were taken aback by the strength of feeling at the demonstration. Then they received a phone call from my parents, who said that they would consider increasing the level of funding if the A&E unit was saved. After that, it didn't take much for them to reconsider their decision.'

'Wow.' Ruby stared at him. 'It pays to have family in high places, doesn't it?' She leaned towards him and nestled into the circle of his arms. 'So you phoned your brother about coming to stay at the house…that was a step in the right direction towards getting your family together, wasn't it?'

His mouth curved. 'More than a step. Robert said he was thinking about setting up a base nearer to London. He loves Scotland, but the children are of an age where they'll be starting secondary school soon, and he and his wife want to bring them back here. They'll keep the house in Scotland as a holiday home and live for a while on our family estate. He said he wants to keep in touch with me on a regular basis.'

'I'm really pleased for you, Sam. It's what you wanted, isn't it?'

He nodded. 'Robert also wants to meet this wonderful woman who's been my inspiration over these last few months.'

'Hmm. I can't wait to meet your family. I wonder how the boys will take to the Shetland ponies? Most children love them on sight.'

He studied her, his blue-grey eyes gleaming with love and desire. 'More to the point, perhaps we ought to start issuing wedding invitations right away. They'll need as much notice as they can get if we're to be married this side of Christmas.'

Her lips parted in a soft smile as she gazed up at him. 'Before Christmas? Is that what you want?'

'Oh, yes,' he said on a positive note. 'I want to make you my bride, and I don't want to wait a minute longer than I have to.'

'I think we're talking commitment with a capital C,' she said on a husky laugh. 'Are you quite sure you're ready for that?'

'Quite sure,' he murmured, folding her into his arms and kissing her soundly. 'Let me show you exactly how committed I am.'

Ruby snuggled into his embrace. She was exactly where she wanted to be…for a lifetime.

MEDICAL™ 2-in-1

Coming next month

THE NURSE'S BROODING BOSS
by Laura Iding

Dr Brock Madison can't believe Elana Shultz works in his new A&E department! Even though she's a daily reminder of his troubled past, Brock simply wants to spend the rest of his life with this nurse in a million – if only Elana will let him in…

EMERGENCY DOCTOR AND CINDERELLA
by Melanie Milburne

When charismatic Eamon Chapman discovers the vulnerable beauty his co-worker Erin Taylor hides behind a prim and proper persona, he finds himself wanting to give this innocent doctor the fairytale happy-ever-after she truly deserves!

CITY SURGEON, SMALL TOWN MIRACLE
by Marion Lennox

Dr Maggie Croft's decision to have her late husband's baby has left her juggling pregnancy with the care of a small town community! Maggie can't afford any distractions, until the arrival of irresistibly gorgeous Max Ashton changes her mind…

BACHELOR DAD, GIRL NEXT DOOR
by Sharon Archer

When single dad Luke Daniels returns to Port Cavill, Dr Terri Mitchell remembers him all too well! Soon Terri has fallen for Luke and his young daughter, but can she convince this doctor to let her heal his troubled heart?

On sale 2nd April 2010

MEDICAL™

Single titles coming next month

A BABY FOR THE FLYING DOCTOR
by Lucy Clark

Doctor Phemie Grainger prides herself on her cool resolve –
until a chance encounter with her professional idol,
Gil Fitzwilliam, throws her into turmoil! As she starts to fall
for the English doctor's charm, Phemie can't help
wondering if, with Gil at her side, her dreams of holding
her very own baby might one day come true…

NURSE, NANNY…BRIDE!
by Alison Roberts

Nurse Alice Palmer's world is turned upside down
when the new A&E consultant is none other than her
teenage crush, Andrew Barrett! The attraction she feels
to him is hard to deny, so when Alice becomes part-time
nanny to his beautiful little girl, it's as if fate has dealt
her the most remarkable hand of all…

On sale 2nd April 2010

Available at WHSmith, Tesco, ASDA, Eason and all good bookshops.
For full Mills & Boon range including eBooks visit
www.millsandboon.co.uk

MILLS & BOON® ROMANCE

is proud to present

Jewels of the Desert

Deserts, diamonds and destiny!

The Kingdom of Quishari: two rulers, with hearts as
hard as the rugged landscape they reign over,
are in need of Desert Queens…

When they offer convenient proposals, will they
discover doing your duty doesn't have to
mean ignoring your heart?

Sheikh Rashid and his twin brother Sheikh Khalid
are looking for brides in…

ACCIDENTALLY THE SHEIKH'S WIFE
And
MARRYING THE SCARRED SHEIKH
by Barbara McMahon
in April 2010

MILLS & BOON® ROMANCE

is proud to present

THE BRIDES OF BELLA ROSA

Romance, rivalry and a family reunited

Lisa Firenze and Luca Casali's sibling rivalry has torn apart the quiet, sleepy Italian town of Monta Correnti for years…

Now, as the feud is handed down to their children, will history repeat itself? Can the next generation undo their parents' mistakes and reunite their families?

Or are there more secrets to be revealed…?

The saga begins in May 2010
with

BEAUTY AND THE RECLUSIVE PRINCE
by Raye Morgan

and

EXECUTIVE: EXPECTING TINY TWINS
by Barbara Hannay

Don't miss this fabulous sequel to
BRIDES OF BELLA LUCIA!

millsandboon.co.uk Community

Join Us!

The Community is the perfect place to meet and chat to kindred spirits who love books and reading as much as you do, but it's also the place to:

- **Get the inside scoop from authors about their latest books**
- **Learn how to write a romance book with advice from our editor**
- **Help us to continue publishing the best in women's fiction**
- **Share your thoughts on the books we publish**
- **Befriend other users**

Forums: Interact with each other as well as authors, editors and a whole host of other users worldwide.

Blogs: Every registered community member has their own blog to tell the world what they're up to and what's on their mind.

Book Challenge: We're aiming to read 5,000 books and have joined forces with The Reading Agency in our inaugural Book Challenge.

Profile Page: Showcase yourself and keep a record of your recent community activity.

Social Networking: We've added buttons at the end of every post to share via digg, Facebook, Google, Yahoo, technorati and de.licio.us.

www.millsandboon.co.uk

2 FREE BOOKS
AND A SURPRISE GIFT

We would like to take this opportunity to thank you for reading this Mills & Boon® book by offering you the chance to take TWO more specially selected books from the Medical™ series absolutely FREE! We're also making this offer to introduce you to the benefits of the Mills & Boon® Book Club™—

- **FREE home delivery**
- **FREE gifts and competitions**
- **FREE monthly Newsletter**
- **Exclusive Mills & Boon Book Club offers**
- **Books available before they're in the shops**

Accepting these FREE books and gift places you under no obligation to buy, you may cancel at any time, even after receiving your free books. Simply complete your details below and return the entire page to the address below. You don't even need a stamp!

YES Please send me 2 free Medical books and a surprise gift. I understand that unless you hear from me, I will receive 5 superb new stories every month including two 2-in-1 books priced at £4.99 each and a single book priced at £3.19, postage and packing free. I am under no obligation to purchase any books and may cancel my subscription at any time. The free books and gift will be mine to keep in any case.

Ms/Mrs/Miss/Mr _____ Initials _____

Surname _____

Address _____

_____

_____ Postcode _____

Send this whole page to: Mills & Boon Book Club, Free Book Offer, FREEPOST NAT 10298, Richmond, TW9 1BR